The Galileans

By

Robert Holladay

With Gratitude

To my wife who walks with me on my journey.

Table of Contents

Other books by Robert Holladay that can be found on Amazon Kindle:

Beyond the Jordon, Galilee of the Gentiles.

Matthew 4:15 - excerpt from the Holy Bible

Preface

In 28 AD, three Galileans; Nathanael of Cana, Herod Antipas, and John the Baptizer become interwoven with each other's destinies through an itinerate preacher from Nazareth called Jesus, whose miraculous healings and preaching throughout the Galilee area electrified the common Jewish people. Nathanael who at first was a follower of John would eventually become a disciple of Jesus. John the Baptizer would be beheaded by Herod Antipas who then would help play a part later with Pontius Pilate in condemning Jesus to death. But well before he is crucified, unbeknownst to them, these three men's paths would cross in defining ways that set the stage for this drama to unfold.

These then are the Galileans; John the Baptizer who has just begun his call to the people of Israel to repent of their sins and be baptized; Herod Antipas, although having been ruler of Galilee for thirty-one years, is now forced to work with the new Roman Prefect, Pontius Pilate in order to placate his ruler and keep his job; and a little-known follower of John named Nathanael who unknowingly runs headlong into the storm of a new way of life through a different person altogether. And they all have one thing in common; Jesus of Nazareth who would soon begin his ministry of healing and preaching of the kingdom of God.

All these beginnings will come to head in the small insignificant region of the Roman Empire called Galilee.

Map of Galilee and Surrounding Region

Prologue –

The Wedding at Cana

"I can't believe they've run out of wine," moaned Zavan as he and his brother Daniel came walking quickly into the large spacious house, both looking worried.

"It wasn't my fault," whispered Daniel as they stopped near the courtyard, his eyes dancing around looking for the head waiter and trouble. It wasn't the first time they had crossed paths with this man and each time they had come out on the short end. Barak had no tolerance for mess ups even if they were his own. "I told Barak that the jars were not full but he ignored me as he always does."

"Shush," whispered Zavan elbowing his brother slightly. "It doesn't matter because we will both get the blame anyway. You know how he hates us."

Zavan's mind quickly raced back a few months before when he had been beaten by Barak for dropping a wine jar. The assistant waiter had used a cane on him and for three days he had not been able to walk. His brother arguing that he had been lucky he had not lost his job or worse been thrown in prison, either which would have been fully justified. The man had a wicked temper as he had shown before on many occasions and Zavan was not relishing the chewing out he was about to get. His day had started out badly enough when his daughter of three had fallen out of their cart and had broken her arm. He couldn't afford to see the local physician whom he owed money to from a miscarriage, not a month before. And now this disaster was looming before him and could mean his job.

A moment later, one of the stewards came in and motioned to the two men to come with him. Zavan glanced at his brother looking for answers as to where they were being led but all he got was a shrug and raised eyebrows. The three men walked across the courtyard past a number of guests who stood around the room drinking wine and eating all sorts of food from fine silver plates. The smells from the roasted meat filled his nostrils but he ignored it although it had been weeks since he had had a good meal. Finally, they came to a small room which was full of odd items, including six stone water jars stacked against the back wall. They were being stored in crates for some sort of ceremonial purpose Zavan knew but he had never seen them used before.

"You see these stone jars?" snapped the steward pointing against the far wall.

Both men nodded as if to say yes. "Well get them out and bring them over to the pool, and do it quickly if you don't want to be beaten."

"What do you reckon we're doing this for?" Daniel asked after the waiter had left. He lifted one of the jars up against his chest and carefully cradled it in his arms before wobbling out the door. The long ornate jar was as heavy as it was cumbersome.

"Don't know, but I can tell you these things are awful weighty for being empty," complained his brother as he hobbled past Zavan carrying the heavy load securely in his arms towards the pool.

Three times they did this until all the stone jars lay next to the large pool which was situated squarely in the center of the massive room. An opening in the roof allowed water to fall in thereby refreshing the pool when it rained. The tiled floor depicting a prowling leopard shimmered in greens and blues at the bottom of the pool and looked to move as a slight breeze wisped through the room rippling the water. Standing next to the assistant waiter Barak, Daniel noted, was another man that he had seen around the wedding feast the last few days but had never heard much from. Although fairly young he was obviously an important person as he most often sat with the head of the household and family during meals with whom Daniel thought was his mother. The two brothers, now finished with their job stepped cautiously back against the wall and waited, expecting to be excused.

"Fill the jars up with water," said the man standing next to Barak. Both brothers shocked at receiving orders from this stranger glanced over at Barak for confirmation.

"Do what the man says," Barak barked at them. "And hurry."

It took some time to fill the jars with water as each held over thirty gallons and it took both of them all their strength to lift them out of the pool once they filled the jars. At last, they had completed their job and they again backed away, heading as they did to the street entrance door, now hoping to really be excused and back to unloading the cart they had left out in the alley.

"You, come back here," said the stranger to Daniel who winced when he saw that he was being pointed at. He walked over to the jars half expecting to have to haul them someplace else and as he did so he glanced back at his brother wondering why he hadn't been called also.

"Draw some out and take it to the head waiter," the man commanded calmly.

Daniel couldn't help glancing up at the man who was giving all these orders and wanted to say 'who are you' but of course valued his life too much and instead kept his mouth shut. He looked around for a goblet or a cup and saw many unused clay cups sitting on a large table for the guest to drink wine from. He stepped over to the table and picked one up. It was heavier than he thought it would be and reckoned it would hold at least a pint or so. Then he leaned the jar over slightly and poured the water out into the cup, except it was no longer water, but had somehow turned into wine.

Daniel almost dropped the cup as he watched the wine fill up inside it. Sweat began to bead on his forehead and he glanced up at the stranger who had been doing all the commanding but he wasn't even paying attention, but instead was talking to the steward. Once the cup was finished he leaned the jar back onto its base and then looked up to see who had seen the water turned to wine but no one was paying any attention. He felt his hand trembling in fear with the knowledge of what had just happened. He thought seriously of dropping the cup and running but decided that would not be in his best interest. Instead, he gawked blinking at the red substance and wished he was somewhere else.

"The head waiter's over in the pantry," said Barak pointing his finger across the room to a large opening near the stairs. "Now do as you've been told and take it to him."

Daniel slowly made his way around the pool and over to the pantry where he saw the head waiter arguing with another steward; his arms whipping about as if he were about to break someone's neck. As he grew closer the head waiter saw him and stopped the tirade but Daniel could tell that he was still fuming.

"What is it?" he bellowed loudly, veins beating against his forehead and sweat pouring down the side of his face.

"I was told to bring you this," he gasped, barely able to speak as held out the cup to the head waiter.

"Well what is it?" he asked again this time even louder.

Daniel was a mess; his mouth was bone dry, his hands still quivered and he now had to relieve himself and all he could think about was that this cup he had in his hands was really water but looked to be wine. "It is wine, sir," he explained raspingly. "I think you are supposed to taste it. It's a new batch."

The head waiter took the cup and stared into it not convinced of its contents. "Where did you get it?" he asked suspiciously. "I was told that we were all out."

"I am not sure," Daniel lied as he wasn't about to tell him what he had just witnessed. In fact, he wasn't very sure that he even knew what he had witnessed.

11

Appearing irritated and flustered the head waiter took the cup, sloshed it around a few times and then took a healthy drink of it. Immediately his eyes opened wide and a pleasant smile came to his mouth. "This is very good," he said smacking his lips. "Where did you say you got it?" he asked taking another drink as if the first wasn't real.

Daniel thought quickly as to how to answer the simple question that wasn't so simple to answer. "You will have to ask the man over by the pool. He's the one who made it."

"Well come on then, let's go see. If there's enough of this to go around then my hide has been saved."

As they came around the pool he noted that the bridegroom and the woman he thought was the mother were now standing next to the stranger that had done this, and they were chatting. The head waiter walked up to them and bowed deeply holding the cup in both of his hands as if it were something important he was about to show them.

Daniel had since moved back to the wall and next to his brother's side. He leaned back against the wall and clenched his fist tightly and closed his eyes.

"Did you see that?" he whispered poking his brother in the side with his elbow still overwhelmed at what he had seen.

"No, I didn't see anything."

"Yes, you did," grumbled Daniel turning to look at his brother. "You had too. We filled up the water jars with water together and then when I poured out the water it was changed into wine. You had to have seen it."

"Yea, I saw that but I didn't see anything happen. What made it change?"

That was Daniel's conundrum. He had no idea how it had happened, just that it had happened. And who in the world was going to believe him? He looked back at the exchange going on and wondered who this man was that had done such a marvelous thing.

The head waiter smiled waving one of his hands at the jars. Then Daniel heard him say to the bridegroom. "Everyone serves good wine first, and then when people have drunk freely, an inferior one; but you have kept the good wine until now."

The waiter looked confused but was delirious at what had happened after taking a drink from the jars himself and tasting its goodness. "This is excellent," he said in wonder as to where it had come from.

"It was that man," said Daniel a while later as they walked out into the street with his brother to continue unloading the meat cart.

"Which man," asked Zavan?

"The one who told us to fill the jars up with water," he answered frustrated with his brother. He had quit unloading and was leaning against the cart still flabbergasted at what had happened. "He was the one who did it, I know it."

"Did what," spat Zavan as he threw a pig's head into a sack. "I saw nothing."

13

Daniel grabbed his brother by the shoulder. "Yes you did," he said savagely. "You saw everything. He turned that water into wine."

Zavan grabbed his brother's hand and wrenched it from his arm. "No, I didn't," he said one last time. "I saw nothing and neither did you. Do you want us both to be thrown out of town to live with the wild people and animals on the outside?"

"No," Daniel answered miserably.

"Well if you keep this up that is where we will be. Now get to work, we have loads of this meat to get inside."

His brother said nothing but shook his head back and forth in a daze. "Who was that man?" he asked himself once again. "And what kind of person could do such a thing?"

That night Daniel finally built up the courage to tell his wife what had happened. He had wanted to tell her all evening but had not had the chance. But finally, he just let it all out. She listened to him in silence, and once finished she felt his head, smelled his breath and then turned back towards the fire where a pot of stew boiled in a black pot. "Call the kids dear," was all she said.

Chapter 1 - Herod Antipas

29 AD

Antipas was tense. The muscle controlling his lip had begun twitching and he was unable to make it stop. When this happened he became irritable and that was how he had begun his day. His wife, Herodias, who sat across the table peering at him while he peeled a couple of quail eggs, knew it and left him alone although she thought he was being trivial. After all, this man Pilate who would be at their door soon had no more authority than her husband had. In all reality, he was just a tax man for Rome whereas her husband actually ran the province. A province by the way, that he had inherited from his father Herod the Great which should have with it the title of King, except that the Romans refused to give it to him which just added insult to injury. She took a short sip of her yogurt and winced slamming the small wooden bowl full of the liquid to the floor making her husband jump up in his chair.

"Abada," she shrieked loudly looking around for her servant girl. "Are you trying to poison me?" she yelled again. The young girl appeared instantly on the patio, her head bowed as low as she could get it and was instantly greeted by a larger bowl of the same liquid slamming into her shoulder splashing the runny substance all over her plain white garment.

"How many times have I told you to add plenty of Pomegranates to the yogurt? This taste like spoiled goat milk. Do I need to whip you again?" she said screeching at the girl.

"Leave her alone," grumbled Antipas as he wiped his mouth with the back of his hand. Suddenly he realized the twitching on his lip had stopped. He glanced at the youth who was now crouching and visibly shaken. Her short stature made her look even smaller against the immense mosaic tiled floor. He had always thought that she had been a good servant as far as servants went. "I don't know why you keep belittling her, the poor girl. She is so afraid of you that she can't do anything right."

Herodias was now standing over her, her arms on her hips. This was a stance that she seemed to favor over any other when about to tear into one of her servants. He watched her halfheartedly out of the corner of his eye. These eggs he adored and preferred them not to be eaten while she fought with her servants. What he wouldn't give for a few peaceful days without his wife blowing up about something or other.

"Well I'll show her," she said spitefully. "I will sell you next time we go into Tiberius. Maybe your next owner can make something of you. Now clean this up and then get out of my sight."

The girl stammered some sort of apology and headed for the door but not before Herodias kicked her with her bare foot. "Unpleasant girl," she hissed before sitting down at the table again.

16

"Why don't you go take a bath and get cleaned up? Our guest will be arriving sometime this morning and I want you looking ravishing for him."

Now Herodias turned on her husband. "Do you think showing off your wife will help appease the Romans?" she said in the same ugly scowl.

"No," he laughed. "I am just being a good host. Now run along while I prepare my scrolls. He's going to want to know where we stand this year and I will not disappoint him."

Most of the morning had been spent already working with his servants preparing an accurate account as to how much grain and other foods had been shipped to Rome this last year. Antipas knew that Pilate would know those numbers and he wanted to get off on a good footing with the new Roman Prefect by showing him he also knew. Antipas had had a very good, and just as importantly a peaceful, relationship with Valerius Gratus, the previous Roman Prefect, and there was no reason why this should be any different. Valerius had been pleasant as long as the taxes came in on time and there was plenty of wine to drink. Antipas saw no reason why this should change with the new Prefect.

He placed the thick duck quill back on the table and stretched. "This should be fine, Antonio," he said to his clerk, dismissing him with a yawn. "I am comfortable that our new Prefect will be pleased with these numbers. They have increased every year since I have been Tetrarch of Galilee and Perea, which should please anyone."

With his work done and a full stomach from his delightful breakfast, he was contented. A nice gentle northern breeze was blowing off of the Sea of Galilee and it soothed his bones. He had been having headaches all week long in anticipation of this meeting but now they were gone and he was in the best frame of mind he had been in a while. New buildings in his new city of Tiberius were going up it seemed almost daily and people continued to pour in. Soon his new city would rival Caesarea with its lavish homes and busy markets and with an Amphitheatre that when completed he was told would be as large as any on this side of the Mediterranean. Maybe Pilate would make this his base instead of Caesarea, he speculated smiling to himself. Of all the new cities he had built, including Sepphoris and Betharamphtha this new city of Tiberius was his crown jewel. If he couldn't impress Pilate with this, he wouldn't be able to impress him at all.

It was mid-afternoon before his guards announced that the Roman entourage was approaching his residence and would soon be on them. Immediately his household servants began to dart here and there setting up tables of fruits and meats on the patio for their new guests. His wife as always supervised the servants with an iron fist and woe to the servant that was caught not minding their job for they would find themselves under the wrath of a cruel woman.

Something caught Antipas' eye and glancing up he saw a falcon snatch a pigeon in midair above the rooftop, feathers flying everywhere. "I hope that's a good omen, Herodias," he said beaming lightly.

"What is," she replied shifting plates and platters from where the servants had set them so that they looked to be more symmetrical. She hated tables that looked like they were thrown together without the slightest thought and made it a point to chastise the head steward for such sloppy work.

"A falcon just seized a pigeon out of the air. It is a sign from the gods. I will seize the initiative against Pilate as the falcon did the pigeon."

"Unless you're the pigeon," she spat back at him while filling a decanter of his favorite red wine near the meats.

Antipas ignored the slight and slid on his white toga which his servant had just handed to him. "Ah, my dear," he said back to her. "You always have such a negative way of looking at things. You must get that from your father. Now smile and act cheery for our guest. Hopefully, they won't stay for more than a few days and then all will be back to normal."

Well trained and handsomely dressed servants entered the palace carrying untold numbers of chest and dressers which quickly filled the outer courtyard. As much as Herodias would have liked to have made some order out of the confusion Antipas would not let her. "You are not a head servant who looks after baggage," he said softly his arm lock tightly around hers so that she could not move. "I do not want the representative of Rome to see my wife carrying on like one."

All of Antipas' confidence in the falcon sign left him as he saw Pilate enter through the double doors of the courtyard. It was obvious who he was by the way he looked and held himself. He was nothing like Valerius Gratus who had been short, fat and bald and always had a scowl on his face. No, he thought, this man was a true Roman, exuding confidence and power and Antipas was suddenly worried that he might be an oppressor. Like Antipas, he wore a beautiful white toga that hung to his knees but this one bore a reddish-purple band on the lower edge that identified his position. The ensemble was tied firmly by a gold sash.

"He looks magnificent," Antipas whispered to his wife who was giving hand signs to her head servant who was trying her best to keep things orderly.

"He looks like a rich Roman to me," she answered as quietly but not really paying him any much attention. He was just a man who dressed well and she could care less.

The man was taller than Antipas with a slim waist and large shoulders. He wore his graying hair in the style of the Romans; short and curly, with a short lightly salted beard prominently displayed only under his wide full mouth. "I wonder which one is his wife?" he asked more of himself than his wife for she was still busy pointing to her servants and was not minding him.

"Pontius Pilate," Antipas called out as calmly as he could when the man was finally just a few feet away.

Pilate's eyes, dark and cold, were locked hard on his. There was a slight smile but Antipas was not sure if it was genuine or forced. Then suddenly within an instant, Pilate's demeanor changed catching Antipas off guard. A large smile full of white teeth followed by outstretched arms greeted Antipas and relieved him of his anxiety.

"Antipas," he answered cheerfully. "It is such a pleasure to be here in this beautiful city."

"And the might and glory of Rome be with you," replied Antipas.

Pilate smiled at the compliment. "It is indeed a pleasure to be here with you at long last," he said. "I have been so busy in Caesarea trying to get my arms around the issues in this province that I have not had the time to come see you. Please forgive me."

Antipas smiled deeply. "There is nothing to forgive. I can't even imagine what you are going through. But more of that later." He turned to point at Herodias. "Let me introduce you to my wife, Herodias."

Antipas was afraid that the introduction of his wife might not go well since it was because of her that he had divorced his first wife, the daughter of King Aretas IV, a friend, and ally of Rome whom now held a deep grudge against Antipas for hurting his daughter. He watched Pilate's eyes for any hint of displeasure but found none.

"It is indeed my pleasure," he said warmly taking her hand and squeezing it lightly. Herodias was still unimpressed. "And now may I introduce my wife Claudia," he said with an outstretched hand towards the woman next to him.

Claudia said nothing, smiled slightly, and then bowed her head a notch at Antipas but did not even look at Herodias. Then she yawned. Pilate ignored the yawn and turned towards the baggage carriers who were setting down boxes, crates, chests and dressers that had been brought in. There appeared to Antipas enough storage to keep him in Tiberius for half a year and knew that Herodias must be steaming.

"Well, what should we do with all this," asked Pilate swinging his arms around in a circle as to encompass everything. "It appears we brought everything from Caesarea with us."

Antipas laughed. He was growing more comfortable with Pilate by the minute even if his wife was not. The rumors had been harsh but the man seemed to be pleasant. "Please don't bother with these things," he said pointing around the courtyard. "The servants can get this straight and taken to your rooms. Let us go to the terrace where we have some fine wine and meats awaiting you."

"That sounds welcoming my friend. It has been a hard ride and I am famished."

With a silver goblet in his hand, Pilate walked along the tables sampling bits and pieces of meats and cheeses. He licked his fingers after having tasted a piece of the fat of the tail of a sheep in which he took a second helping. "Delicious," he said sincerely. "I'm not sure I have had this before."

"The fat of the sheep tail," answered Herodias softly. "It is a delicacy here since we have so few sheep. I will have my Steward tell your servants how to prepare it."

"Yes," he quickly replied. "I remember now. We had some in Ephesus, didn't we my dear?"

His wife murmured in agreement but ate none. She was nearly as tall as he but much thinner. She seemed even taller with her toga snuggly tied under her breast so that the rest of the material fell fully to her feet. Her hair was graying like his and worn back behind her head with a beautiful engraved silver comb shaped like a peacock. She was strikingly beautiful he noted, befitting of a wife of such an important husband. Suddenly Antipas felt embarrassed for divorcing his first wife for Herodias. She had been a beauty like Pilate's wife but had whined so much that he simply one day sent her home back to her father after having met and stolen Herodias from his half-brother.

"You are not hungry, your highness," asked Antipas politely to Claudia?

She did not speak but instead looked to her husband who spoke for her. "It takes some time to get used to your rich foods," he answered as he continued to walk along the massive table that stretched across the terrace. Suddenly he stopped and pointed. "Here you are, my dear. Olives." He turned towards Antipas and smiled. "How Claudia loves olives. And look my love; not only olives but grapes and figs. You are in Rome by god," he laughed.

Antipas smiled and laughed also with delight at pleasing Pilate and even better his wife, who had spoken very little since arriving. Herodias, on the other hand, frowned at the tall stately woman and would have liked to have shoved one of the precious quails that cost an arm and leg to buy down her throat. "Oh, how nice," she said instead. "Please help yourselves to whatever most pleases you."

Pilate sat next to Antipas with a goblet in his hand and a half finished flattened goose smothered in garlic and peppers before him. He had just finished chewing on a stuffed turtledove egg. "Delicious," he said sounding very sincere to Antipas as he chased the egg with his wine.

"Which?" Antipas asked smiling. "The turtledove or the wine."

Pilate returned the smile. "Why both of course," he said. "You set a very respectable table here in Tiberius I must admit. I trust the baths are as agreeable."

"Only the finest," he replied hoping that Pilate would feel the same way.

"Good. Then let's meet in the morning and try your baths. I would like to speak a bit about our visit if we could. Would that be agreeable?"

Pilate rose with his hands stretched out to Claudia before Antipas had a chance to reply and so he decided the question needed no answer and remained quiet. The servants showed the guest their quarters as Antipas and Herodias left for their room and undressed in quite. The cool sea breeze continued to blow nicely through the windows but it wasn't enough to relieve the stress in the room. Antipas, always thinking, looked out over his city wondering how the beginning of the visit went and if he had scored any points with the new Prefect.

"He's dangerous," said Herodias as she slipped under the covers.

The words surprised Antipas so much that he couldn't think of how to reply. He turned to her sitting up and looking even more surprised than he sounded. "Why in the world would you say that?"

"Because he's a creature of Rome," she responded, her words sounding sharp and hateful. "He's a spider waiting to catch its prey in his net, and you my dear just in case you haven't figured it out, are not the spider."

"But sweetheart," Antipas said still off-guard. "He has no reason to catch me in a web. We are equals. And besides, he needs me. I'm the one who keeps the peace and raises his precious taxes."

"Well I don't trust him one bit," Herodias shot back at him immediately. "Neither do I trust that pretentious wife of his. Did you not notice that not once did he call you by your title? You're a king and he treated you like a servant."

Antipas shook his head in disbelief. "Of course, he didn't dear. He had no reason to. My title just didn't come up in the conversation."

"Well, I can assure you that they are here for one purpose and one purpose only; to get rich so that they can move back to Rome in the style they are accustomed to. And you are only involved in as much as you help him achieve his goal. You may think you are equals but you are just a pawn of Rome."

Antipas just stared at his wife not knowing how to answer that. She was probably right about his wanting to get rich but then so did every other Prefect or Governor who ran a province for Rome. They all had the same goal. Why not? But Pilate showed no hint to him of being antagonistic towards him nor did he seem to be mistrustful of his rule. He was about to say this when Herodias rolled over offering her back to him which, of course, meant that it was the end of the conversation and that she would not listen to anything else he had to say.

"Well, I am to meet him at the baths tomorrow and we shall see."

Not feeling tired Antipas walked out onto the terrace and poured himself another cup of wine. It was much cooler now and he felt good. Despite what his wife thought, he enjoyed Pilate's company and felt as if the two got off to a good start. Herodias didn't know a thing about the political world and was just being apprehensive about the new Prefects role. After all, he assured himself, Pilate had no authority over Galilee or Perea. He was the protectorate of Judea for Rome and although his position and power probably overlapped other provinces some, that would be the extent of it. They would work together to maintain peace and make sure that Rome's taxes were collected. That would be all.

He took another hard swallow and looked up into the night sky hoping for a sign, but saw none.

Chapter 2 - Pontius Pilate

Antipas was there at the baths the next day well before Pilate showed up. He wanted to make sure that the water temperature was correct and that there were plenty of fruits and nuts and good wine. He made sure that he had at least three large amphorae of wine especially the honey-pepper red wine made from his large vineyard outside of Sepphoris to the west. The dry air and rocky slopes were perfect for the grapes he grew and he worked very hard at making them one of the best blends in the area. He was very proud of his vineyards and hoped to sell some of his stock to Rome through Pilate. It would do both of them good to have a small partnership to seal their relationship during his stay.

After his bath, Pilate entered the pool where Antipas waited. The water was perfect he knew but wanted Pilate to say something first. "You have made a first class bath house here in Tiberius Tetrarch," Pilate commented as he lay against the tiles and sipped on his wine.

Antipas would have to remember to tell Herodias that Pilate used his title, Tetrarch. "I am glad you are pleased," he said. "I have made it a point to at least equal or exceed the baths at Caesarea where you are making your headquarters. We are lucky enough to have dozens of hot springs in the area that feed the baths and make them just about always accessible." He paused for a moment allowing his guest to appreciate what he had said. "Of course, you are always welcome to stay here with us if you prefer."

Pilate really meant what he had said. The tile patterns on the floors and walls were exquisite especially the tiled leopard that lay beneath their feet on the bath floors. He was also impressed with how clean everything was and the care they took to make sure the water was perfectly heated. "You may rest assured that I will make this trip often," he said smiling. "If not to bask in your baths, then most definitely we shall be here to drink this marvelous wine. The flavor is incredible."

"It is my own process Prefect. I add a touch of honey to sweeten the flavor. I am glad you like it. I will send a case along with you when you go."

"That is most kind. I would like that very much." Pilate paused for a moment staring at Antipas as if he were sizing him up. "How long have you ruled here for us?" he asked coolly.

Antipas cheerful demeanor suddenly was dashed when he heard Pilate use the words 'for us'. As sudden as that, their equal status had disappeared. "Let me see," he began, trying to keep himself calm under this new scrutiny. "Emperor Augustus installed me as Tetrarch thirty-one years ago or there about." He surely wanted to make it clear to Pilate that it was the Roman emperor who placed him in this province, which validated his position.

Pilate ignored the pedigree. "And in that time, you have had a fairly peaceful reign?"

Antipas nodded. "Yes. More than my half-brother Archelaus had in Judea if that is what you are referring to."

Pilate smiled half laughing. "No, not at all, my friend. Archelaus was a nuisance and not a friend of Rome, as you are. It is good that he is gone. I just wanted to congratulate you on a long successful and peaceful reign."

Antipas continued cautiously putting on a half-smile. "And we thank you, Prefect, for noticing. We have a well-trained force protecting our borders and do not let undesirables into our territory."

Pilate took another sip of wine but did not take his eyes off of Antipas. "There are two things that our emperor requires of you Antipas; peace and grain." He said this sternly as if explaining to a servant how to perform a menial task. "As long as you can assure us of these two things, my friend, Rome will be happy and you may keep your position."

This startled Antipas. He had never been spoken to like this in his thirty-year reign. He, after all, was the rightful heir to this land which was given to him by his father Herod the Great. No one had the right to question his pedigree or had the audacity to suggest that they could allow him to 'keep' his position. "Am I to take that as a warning?" he asked delicately, trying his best to keep from becoming enraged. There would be nothing gained in blowing up before the emperor's appointed emissary.

Pilate let out a deep laugh that surprised Antipas. "Of course not!" he exclaimed. "You are a friend of Rome and we want nothing more of you than a successful reign for as long as you rule here. I personally hope that it is a very long time for I believe we will make a great team; you here in Galilee and me in Judea, or is that Samaria?" He laughed again and finished off his wine with one last slug. "Let's have one more cup of wine to solidify our arrangement, shall we?"

Antipas tried to smile but it was forced. He nodded to his servant to pour more wine while he thought through what was said. "Then the emperor is pleased with our province?" he asked Pilate wondering how much of this talk was from Rome and how much was from Pilate himself.

"Why of course he is pleased. Why wouldn't he be? You just make sure the grain allotment and tax collections keep up with their former pace and all will be well. I have plenty to take care of in Jerusalem. But let us finish with this talk of taxes and governance. Let us talk of other things manlier. When can we go hunting? I would love to bag a lion."

They spoke of eating mouthwatering wild boar and of hunting and wine and tall lanky women and all the building that Antipas had done in Sepphoris and Betharamphtha, as well as Tiberius, which he was pleased to share, was a magnificent city and his crown achievement. After spending a short time in the steam room and then cooling off in the second pool they dried, dressed and then began their walk through the city streets to the forum which Pilate wanted to see. It was just a short distance from the baths which were near the city gates of the Roman city to the forum. As they walked, Antipas pointed out the theater. "It will hold seven thousand when it is finished," he said proudly. "I hope you will be able to come back when it is complete and enjoy our entertainment. My steward assures me we will be delighted."

Little was said as they walked on further but Antipas noted that Pilate looked impressed. Finally, after passing through several streets of merchants and vendors selling everything from wine to freshly baked bread they approached the forum plaza which was an enormous area fully tiled with a twelve-foot wide portico around the outer rim which opened into the government city buildings. Pilate immediately noticed more merchants gathering in clumps doing business here and there while a juggler performed for a group of citizens laughing and clapping in one corner.

Directly in front of them a large rectangular fountain with a naked woman covering her nakedness stood surrounded by sprouting water from four identical dolphins at each corner. "Isn't that a statue of Venus?" Pilate asked sounding curious upon approaching the fountain? It stood near the edge of the plaza on the far side of the Jewish synagogue.

"Why yes," answered Antipas delighted to show off his beautiful marble fountain that had been carved by a Roman sculpture.

Pilate ran his hand along the marble then nonchalantly added, "I thought a Roman Goddess would have been forbidden by your religion."

"In respect for Rome and her gods, we adore Venus," explained Antipas proudly. "Like Rome itself, we would like Tiberius to be open to all gods."

"But isn't that against Jewish law?" he asked. "And wouldn't that upset your Jewish hierarchy?"

This made Antipas uncomfortable. "Well," he began thinking quickly. "It has caused some grief I must be honest. But so has the cemetery along the east side of the city and some foods being sold by the merchants. You cannot have a vibrant growing city without having to make compromises, and unfortunately, because of it, I have had to force some to inhabit the city despite them. But you must understand that both are necessary to show that we welcome Rome and all it brings to the world."

"But why Venus? Why not Mars or Zeus?" he asked.

Antipas was a little embarrassed to tell Pilate the truth but he decided he must. If they were to work together they must be honest. "I'm afraid I must confess my wife Herodias is enamored with Venus. She paid for the statue out of her own dowry so it was hard to refuse."

That intrigued Pilate. "Does Herodias have a large dowry?" he asked innocently.

It bothered Antipas that Pilate would ask a question about the wealth of his wife so he looked for a way to dodge the question. "Well she was the granddaughter of Herod the Great you know," he answered skillfully.

Pilate nodded, seemingly to accept his explanation for he didn't comment any further. He knew that Antipas was also a grandson of Herod by a different mother but had no reason to bring that bit of his history up. "It is beautiful," he said after having walked most of the city. "How is it governed?"

"Well, I, of course, make most major decisions," answered Antipas still upset about his inquiries in Herodias's fortune. "But we also have a small council of roughly 10 members who at any given time make the day to day judgments. I stole this idea from my first wife's father. It has worked well for us so far."

Later that night Antipas sat with his wife on their veranda after their guest had retired. He sipped on a cup of wine with his toga still on and she sat on a lounger near him in a silk sadin which was needed on this warm night. They hadn't had any time to speak with each other since he had come back from the city with Pilate. Now he waited for her to say something so that he could judge her defiance. He didn't want to argue this night with her but knew it probably would end up that way.

"So what did he say," she finally asked in her typical impertinent voice which he had grown to hate.

He thought about how to answer for it depended on which way he went as to how bad she would respond. "Quite pleasant," he said knowing that she wouldn't believe him. "We had a wonderful conversation in the baths and then I took him around the city. He was very complimentary at what we have done."

"Well, that little snake he carries around with him as a wife doesn't agree with you."

Antipas was shocked that they had discussed anything having to do with how he ran his province. "Why, what did she say," he asked trying to sound as if he didn't really care.

"She said that Rome was ready at any moment to take away all the provinces from the rulers and give it all to Pilate to run. They are tired of the squabbling between the family members, which it seems no one can control."

Nothing like that was conveyed to him by Pilate which bewildered Antipas greatly. "Well, I'm not so sure she has any great connections in Rome which to garner that information so I don't give it much credence."

"Her uncle is a very respected and powerful Senator. But be that as it may, I would watch Pilate like a hawk."

"Well the sooner they leave to go back to Caesarea the better," he said trying to change the subject. "I'm getting tired of his petty nuances about my kingdom."

Herodias laughed. "Well look at you. Aren't you the brave one when he isn't around?"

Antipas looked at her with contempt, rose and left her sitting by herself.

A week later Antipas finally said farewell to Pilate and Claudia. Pilate had received news from Caesarea that there had been a killing of a tax collector in the region and that made Pilate very angry. "I will find out who did this and I will have their head," he said the day he heard of the violence. "This type of thing cannot be tolerated. I hope you understand."

Caesarea was part of Judea which was controlled directly by Rome and thus Pilate, which didn't affect Antipas unless it spread to his territory. Even then Pilate had no real control except to make sure that the grain and taxes were collected on time. But Antipas had been doing that for a long time and knew how to get his tax collectors to get what he wanted without upsetting the merchants too much.

"Well I hope you are successful in catching whoever did this," he answered not really interested but trying to sound so. He had many more soldiers than Pilate had at his disposal but wasn't about to volunteer to lend him any help. He could get out of this mess himself.

Pilate took a drink of his wine and continued. "I will look for you to keep the peace here in Galilee and Perea. These Jews have been flexing their muscles of late and I will have a time keeping them in check. "Do not let me down Antipas. I am counting on you."

Antipas held his tongue for he was confident that he would keep the peace. No one in his province had crossed that line yet and he was sure no one would. Pilate had no idea what he had gotten into when he had become Prefect of Judea. Antipas knew of the anger of his people towards Rome because he has been in the streets and had listened to his people. No one wanted Rome as their ruler but they could live with that as long as the tax man didn't help himself to more than his share. It was all about equality and Antipas made sure his tax collectors understood that. He didn't mind if they took some off the top but he did mind when they stole wholesale from his people. He made a note to himself to check again to make sure his men were honest. They would need to be at least as honest as he would have been.

Pilate left early the next morning and Herodias was ecstatic. She hadn't even gone out to see them off but stayed in her bedroom. "That man will be the death of us all," she exclaimed as they watched the last of the wagons negotiate the narrow gate from her palace window.

Some time later they were sitting on the terrace where breakfast lay on the table. "I don't know why you hate him so much," he said while peeling another egg. Her breakfast lay uneaten on her table and so he had helped himself to one of hers. There was no reason for it to go to waste. "Yes, he's a little brash but it could always be worse. Besides, he will spend most of his time in Judea. You won't have to put up with her for a long time to come. They will keep him busy, mark my words."

"Well good riddance to him and that toad he calls a wife," she spat out. "The less I see of Rome the better. This is our kingdom and as far as I am concerned he is not welcomed back. Your father would not have let them get away with this."

Antipas walked over to his wife at her dressing table and kissed her on the head. Life was much easier when he appeased her, he knew even if it did usurp his authority. "If it pleases you I won't invite him back dear. He really has nothing to do here anyway, so you will probably get your wish."

"Anyway, it is time for me to go see Salome," she said piqued. "I haven't seen my dear child in six months. The poor girl has grown up without her mother and it's your fault. You have kept me here entirely too long."

"Business calls my love and I have had a lot of things to consider here in Tiberius," he said sounding conciliatory but none-the-less firm. "If you want to go along to Machaerus without me and spend the next few months with her then go right ahead, but I have too much to do here and in Sepphoris to take off at this time. Why don't you bring her back here and then we can stay through the winter."

"Not on your life," she said with great conviction. Antipas drew back at the words. She was being such a cow lately that he wasn't so sure he would be glad that she was gone. "Your fiftieth birthday party is in six months and we will have it in Machaerus where all my family is."

He had forgotten about the party and that he had promised her that it would be there if she would come to Tiberius with him. "But I hate Machaerus Herodias. It is so dull there. There is not even a good bath or a decent theater. Why don't we have it here?"

She turned to him in a rage. "Because you promised, and I will not have you go back on your word."

There would be no victory here Antipas knew and so he shrugged his shoulders and grabbed a piece of flat cake and spread some honey on it. "Your right my dear, I have forgotten I promised and I will be there. Why don't you go ahead on without me and I will catch up next month. I promise to be there well before my party."

She smiled for the first time since Pilate had entered into his house. "You are such a good husband. I can't wait to get back and see papa. Will you arrange it for me? I get so lost when it comes to having to get all my stuff packed."

The honey was delicious. Antipas continued to look out the window and wondered what Pilate had in mind for his province and how it would affect him. "Yes dear," he said absentmindedly. "I will take care of it all."

Chapter 3 - John the Baptizer

John awoke to a fly buzzing across his forehead. He brushed it away and searched the skies. The cloudless firmament promised another hot dry dusty day, but it didn't really bother him for that was not why he was here. As he sat up he noticed his companion still asleep and the once hot fire they cooked over last night was all but extinguished. They had eaten their last food, some boiled mutton and several pieces of flatbread, but that didn't bother him either for food would be provided, it always was. But his blanket, which had been his companion now for the last two years, was becoming a problem. It was growing threadbare and in some places, he could see through it, and he could do with another. It would get cold before long and then he would wish he had another.

He stood up, stretched and then walked over to the stream they had slept by splashing the cool water on his face and drinking several mouthfuls. A cormorant walked along the edge looking for breakfast but appeared to see nothing appealing. What little breeze that the climate could muster along the river felt refreshing as it skimmed across the water touching his face ever so slightly where he had just splashed water on himself. Looking across the stream he reckoned it would take less than a day to get to the river and then he would have to make a decision. They had already been thrown out of Bethel, Shilo, Jericho and several other small villages and towns and he was running out of the places to go. With nowhere else to go he would either have to travel up the River Jordon towards the Sea of Galilee or cross over into the district of Perea. Either way, they would finally be out of the dessert and they could find a town that had not seen or heard of him before.

It worried him that he had not found the place where he could deliver his message in peace. No matter where they went the Jewish hierarchy would soon get the word of them and it wouldn't be long before they would be forced out. The message he had received in a dream did not sit well with the elders of the towns. First, they would turn them out of the synagogue, then anyone giving them the shelter or food would be ostracized, and finally the Jews themselves with help from Antipas's frontier guard would forcibly remove them. John was beginning to wonder if he would ever be safe in any town. And if so to whom would he deliver his message?

"Hey there, caught any fish?" yelled Nathanael from back in the camp. "I'm starving," he added as if he hadn't eaten in a week.

John smiled. Nathanael was always worrying about the things of this world. He was a delightful companion, had a deep belief in his religion, but wasn't really on fire with the message. He spent more time looking for a great campsite, gathering food, and securing shelter than he did talking about God. They needed a permanent place where they could focus on the message and not on worldly things. Only then would Nathanael have a chance to concentrate on what was important.

"You have to quit worrying about your next meal," he said, the smile still on his face.

"Well someone does. It's not like we have any money, and we're not very good at begging."

"We're not beggars Nathanael," he said sounding exasperated. "We are preachers. We let God take care of the earthly matters while we bring the people back to God. That's what we do."

"Well, that sounds good unless we haven't had anything to eat in two or three days."

John laughed. "Maybe God gave you to me so as to make sure I don't starve."

Nathanael scoffed. "Well, then I'm not doing too well am I?"

John patted his friend on the back. "Yes, you are. You are doing exactly what God wants you to do. But for now, we need to get moving. I would like to get to the river by this afternoon."

Nathanael walked quietly along the road ignoring John for he was in one of his moods which Nathanael had learned to ignore. For no matter what he said to John he would only receive a grunt in reply which meant little and so he left him alone. The road was well traveled with merchants and bands of families falling in together to make small caravans but they stayed mostly to themselves. Most walked, some rode donkeys or an occasional camel, but once in a while, they would pass by wagons loaded with goods and spices and sacks of barley and wheat for sale. These would be led by armed men on horse and were usually given a wide berth. Roman military, always feared, were rare and royalty was even rarer.

Suddenly John stopped. Nathanael had not made an effort to stay close and so was a distance away when he saw John pause and then walk over to a small caravan which had stopped off the side of the road. Several men were working on a wheel which seemed to have broken a spoke and had slipped off the axle. A number of children were running around making noises but had careful maternal eyes watching them. It was noon and the women were fixing food for the families.

John walked up to the women who were sitting on an enormous rug and were preparing bowls of stew and tearing off bread from large loaves. Other bowls of olives and nuts were arranged before them ready to eat. They looked up at him as he got closer but since a woman would never speak to a stranger first they waited for him to speak. The older women wore veils woven with spectacular colors that protected their heads and faces from the blazing sun.

"My name is John," he said warmly. "I have been sent by God to preach repentance and testify to the light who is coming into the world."

One of the older women who had been tearing bread crossed her arms and peered up at him through the slit in her veil. "What has that to do with us?" she said. "We are Persians, from Decapolis and have many gods. Which one are you referring to?" she asked.

John looked up into the sky. "There is only one true God," he exclaimed rather loudly. "Your gods are created by man, but my God is the creator and ruler of all."

"Why do you bother these women with talks of god?" said a man who appeared from seemingly nowhere but must have been working on the wheel. He was big with a full beard and large powerful looking arms that were made for heavy lifting. He wore no outer garment to conceal his muscular frame and that bothered Nathanael who had just caught up with John. He was not a fighting man and had no desire to get into a tussle with this giant.

"Can't you see that they have work to do?" he continued loudly. "They do not have time to speak of these things. So leave us in peace before my men and I have to chase you off."

To Nathanael's chagrin, John did not back off but instead turned and smiled at the man. "Then I shall speak to you of our God. Have you never heard of Moses and how his God forced the Pharaoh of Egypt to free the Jews in bondage and then when Pharaoh changed his mind he and his men were drowned in the Red Sea, but Moses and the Jews escaped? It was by the power of my God that this was done and you and all your people will see even more miracles when the Son of Man comes. The Messiah will break the yoke of the Romans and set our people free once again."

The tenseness in the man seemed to go away and his tight fists which had been clinched before were now relaxed. Nathanael was glad to see that the strain on his face had turned to a frown for he had been fearful that the man might hit John. "Yes I have heard of this Messiah," he said skeptically; "This King that would lift you Jews out of slavery by throwing out the Romans."

"Yes," barked John. "That is him."

Ha," laughed the big man sarcastically. "That my friend is a bunch of rubbish, for no one can break the yoke that Rome has on the world."

John spat back instantly. "Rome only has a yoke on the world because God lets it. Even your King Cyrus long ago let the Jews return home after seventy years of exile because my God told him to in a dream. And he was the most powerful ruler in the world."

"Then why did your God after bringing them out of Egypt allow your people to go back into bondage?" he argued back at John sounding ever more perturbed. "He doesn't seem like a very good god to me. Does he come and go like the night sky only to have to get you Jews back out of trouble every few hundred years?"

"No," shot back John even louder now almost in the face of the giant. Nathanael wished he would be a bit calmer when he argued with strangers especially men as big as this one was. "But he does punish us when we turn from him and raise idols before him and live in wicked and bad ways. He is a God of love but also one of punishment. And he will punish you for not turning to him. He will judge you and your people if you do not repent."

It was a stalemate which neither wished to back down from and so in order to restore peace Nathanael seized John's arm slowly pulling him back from the confrontation. At first, he held firm but soon let Nathanael pull him away. "He was almost convinced," he told Nathanael after having walked a distance from them. "I could feel it."

"I'm not so sure you were feeling the right vibes," answered Nathanael looking back to make sure they were well away from the caravan. "You have to be careful," he continued. "You could get us into big trouble one day."

John stopped and turned to Nathanael placing his hand on his friend's shoulder and smiled. Suddenly he was no longer confrontational. "What has that to do it as long as we are speaking the truth and telling the message? These are just bodies," he said slapping his friend with his hand. "We should have no fear for God is with us. He will come to our aide."

Nathanael looked bewildered. "I am not so sure God gets into squabbles," he said. "You need to keep the message to the Jews. At least they know what you are talking about."

John shook his head in disagreement. "God is the God of all people, Nathanael. I will talk to whoever will listen, Jew or Greek."

There was no use trying to dissuade him so Nathanael gave up the argument and they continued on. Before long Nathanael noticed reeds towering above the landscape and he knew they were close. "Look," he said to John pointing to the reeds. "The river must be right up ahead."

The road, which was nothing more than a wide dirt path with ruts in it from wagon wheels that had driven this site for centuries, led right to the water and then continued out on the other side. The river, which couldn't have been more than thirty feet across was murky in this area where the caravans crossed daily and seemed to be shallow enough to wade. Further up a bend in the river made it disappear from sight and below them, it drifted aimlessly through the desert for a long time before also disappearing into the landscape. The reeds covered both sides for as far as he could see.

"The River Jordon," John said to no one in particular. "I was here as a young boy with my father but have not been back since. He died when I was very young."

Nathanael knew about John's father Zachariah. There was a folktale about how he was struck deaf by an angel because he wouldn't believe the angel was real and how when John was born he wrote down for the townspeople to see the name John instead of his family name of Zachariah, which would have been the appropriate name to have given the child. Then the story went out that immediately after having written the name his voice came back and everyone was in awe at what had happened. The boy grew into a man and left after his studies to pursue this life of austerity to preach this vision he said had been given to him also by an angel in a dream. As with most old stories Nathanael didn't place much stock in its truthfulness but he guessed that there was something that had happened to have made him change.

"What do you think," asked Nathanael to his friend. "Do we cross or do we go east up the river?"

But John was silent. He just stared at the river, his deep searing eyes fixed on the water flowing past the travelers. Nathanael could tell that something was stirring inside of him. It was something that happened to him periodically and when it did there was nothing to do but wait until whatever he was searching for became clear.

Nathanael watched the travelers as they made their way through the water, crossing from both sides not paying attention to the others but intent on getting to wherever it was that they needed to get to. The sun made him sleepy and so he sat down on a rock and drifted in and out of sleepiness until a while later John finally spoke. "Look at the water Nathanael," he said suddenly and with enough sternness to cause Nathanael to jump up. "You see how it flows?" he almost yelled. "It is the essence of life Nathanael. It is where God wishes me to cleanse his people." He paused for a moment looking more deeply at the water. "Don't you see?" he continued on his excitement growing. "Through this purity, I will wash away their sins and they will be given to them a new life."

Nathanael couldn't see anything but murky water with an occasional stick or leaf floating by. He had known John for a little over a year and had followed him for most of that time but never had he heard him sounding so irrational. How could this muddy milky water cleanse anyone of anything he wondered? For the first time be suddenly felt sorry for his friend. He had been kicked out of so many towns that he had finally given up, and now this is where he would settle?

Then suddenly to Nathanael's amazement John walked down to the river, tied his garment tightly around him and entered the water up to his waist yelling at the top of his voice while throwing his arms out wide as he did. "Repent," he exclaimed. "Repent and be baptized, here in the flowing waters of life."

A hush fell on the passerby's who suddenly stopped and looked up from their tired feet to see this crazy man yelling and swinging his arms at everyone. And then as an afterthought, he pointed his arm and finger at the water. "Come," he screamed at them once more. "Come and receive life." Everyone had stopped and was now staring at this crazed figure. Then a poorly dressed yet clean shaven man who was leading a donkey dropped the bridle and stepped towards John hesitantly. "Who are you?" he asked suspiciously. "Are you the Prophet?"

John looked taken aback and hesitated before answering. "No, I am not the Prophet," he changed his tone and was now speaking slower and less loudly, but just as directly. "I am the voice of one crying out in the desert spoken by the prophet Isaiah who said; 'Prepare the way of the Lord and make straight his paths.'"

Suddenly a middle-aged woman appeared beside the man, this one finely dressed and well spoken. "Then who do you speak of and what should we do?" she asked.

Nathanael was dumbstruck that any of them were paying attention to him at all. John stuck out his hand to the lady beckoning her to him. "What is your name sister?"

She hesitated but then answered. "My name is Joanna. I am from Tiberius."

John motioned for her to come to him. "Even now," he said gently, "the ax lies at the root of the tree. Therefore, every tree that does not produce good fruit will be cut down and thrown into the fire."

Then another man from the middle of the river who had been crossing before John began to yell, shouted out above the crowd earnestly, "Then what should we do?"

"Come and be baptized," John answered even louder so that they all could hear. "Repent and be cleansed, and then produce good fruits as evidence of your repentance." He turned from one to another, his hands beckoning them to come. "Come and be baptized. Repent and God who is all forgiving will forgive you."

Surprisingly the man suddenly moved towards John sloshing through the water as he waded waist deep in the river. There was such intensity in his eyes that it startled Nathanael. He cried out, "Baptize me sir so that I may repent of my sins."

Nathanael was dumbfounded. He had been staring first at the lady and then at the man next to her and now at this man in the river. He couldn't believe that they were suddenly driven to this mad man in the river wanting to be baptized by him. Then he watched as John took the man in his arms and lowered him in the waters saying as he did, "I baptize you in water to wash away your sins." Then after submerging him he pulled the man back up and led him to the shore. "Repent and sin no more," he told him.

As the man crawled up on the shore John stretched out his hand to the woman he had spoken to earlier. "Come sister and be baptized. Repent for the time is at hand and indeed grows near when someone greater than I will come for the salvation of all sins."

Then to Nathanael's wonder, even she waded into the river and was submerged by John. As she came up he couldn't help but notice that her eyes were wide in ecstasy and she was exclaiming something he couldn't understand. And then before she could get to the shore another man came to him, not saying a word but modestly submitting himself to John. And before Nathanael knew what was happening there was a line on the shore waiting to get in.

He was still dumbfounded at what was going on when the lady who had been baptized came up to him. "Are you with the baptizer," she asked softly her hair dripping still from the river's water, her once colorful well-fit dress now soaked.

Nathanael was startled that she asked. He had not said anything to John the entire time and so wondered how she had known. "Yes," he said hesitantly. "He is my friend."

"I thought so for you were looking at him so intently as if you were his protector."

Nathanael did not know how to answer her or even what to say. Things had happened so fast that even he couldn't grasp what was evolving. "I guess," he finally mumbled.

Then she turned and singled to a man who brought over a basket full of items. She opened it and showed Nathanael what was inside. To his amazement, he was looking at nearly a dozen new colorful blankets and other clothing items. "Here, these are yours."

Never before had anyone given them the likes of this. They had received morsels of food which had kept them alive but nothing of this enormity. No one in their right mind would do such a thing. He couldn't believe that this was happening. "Thank you, mam, for the cloaks and blankets," he said hesitantly. "But I will never be able to repay you."

She smiled at him. "I don't want repayment," she said gently. "He has already given me what I want; a hope that we all desperately need." She started to turn and then decided to ask one more question. "What is it that you call him?"

It was a simple question but like everything else that had happened that day, it took him by surprise. "John," he finally said. She smiled and then left and Nathanael watched her as she slowly disappeared into the crowd. Then he looked back into the water to see John surrounded by people who were still coming to him.

Not everyone went to John but many did and continued to do so the rest of the afternoon until almost dark. They seemed to feed on each other's emotions but soon the dusk grew over them and the crowds disappeared and Nathanael yelled at John that he needed to come out so that they could find shelter. John looked tired and hesitated to look around for any last taker but then did as he was told and sloshed towards the bank. As he crawled out of the river he looked at Nathanael's feet.

"What is all that?" he asked looking at the pile of stuff.

"It was her," he exclaimed. "The woman you baptized. Once she found out that I was with you, she overwhelmed me with these clothes and this sack of food. 'I have plenty,' she told me and then said, 'I will pray that God will bless you for what you have done for me this day.' Then she told me that her husband and she were servants in the household of King Herod and had longed to hear these words that you had exclaimed today."

John smiled. "You see Nathanael, I told you that God would provide as long as we never refused to give up."

They camped on a hill on the far side of the river on a flat spot that Nathanael had seen earlier. They now had new blankets and plenty of food and wine and John even had a dry robe that was given to him and a new kethōneth to put on under it. "We have been truly blessed," he said after saying a blessing over the food and then began to eat some nuts and goat cheese. Nathanael chewed on a piece of salted goat meat wrapped in flat bread while chasing it with beer. Both were completely satisfied and before long and they lay back on their new blankets to enjoy the night sky.

"Where are we to go tomorrow," asked Nathanael off the cuff wondering what their next move would be.

"Go?" John asked flabbergasted. "Go," he said again sitting up. "Why nowhere," he exclaimed. "This is where we shall stay. It was the river Nathanael. The river beckoned me to itself as it did to Moses in ancient times and like Moses before me, I was called by God to do his will."

"You wish to stay here at the river?" Nathanael asked in astonishment. "Why we have no shelter and when this food is gone, we will be without."

"God will provide, Nathanael, as he did today."

"But how long can we stay out here in this wilderness?" he asked. "There are a beast and bandits and before long winter will come. We can't just stay here John. Let us find a village or town near here so that at least we will have a roof over our heads."

"No," he said shaking his head emphatically. "I have made up my mind. Can't you see how perfect this place is? God has led me to it. There are no elders to run us off and we will be at peace with everyone. Didn't you see how the people hungered at the sound of God's promises? No, this is where I have been called and this is where I will stay."

Nathanael wasn't as sure as he but he could tell that John was set on staying so he decided not to argue any longer. He peered into the sky as he thought back on the day. So many things had happened and it had affected so many people. He still wasn't sure why all those strangers would let him dunk them in the water just because he had said they needed to.

"What did you mean that someone else who will come to forgive all who have sinned?"

"The Messiah, Nathanael," he said. "I am speaking of the Messiah."

"But the Messiah has been foretold for hundreds of years. I thought it was just a myth; something to hold on to until we can get us a new king."

"But he will be the new king. It is he who will bring salvation to all the lands. I am just baptizing with water, he will baptize with the Holy Spirit."

Nathanael wasn't sure what he had meant about the Holy Spirit and wasn't really interested. He was tired and worried about staying out here for months on end with no shelter. Suddenly he was wondering if John had lost his senses. Why else would anyone want to stay out here in the wild? Maybe he would go scout around to see if he could find somewhere that they would go to rest for a while or to get out of bad weather. He would bring it up on the morrow and see what John thought of his idea.

But John was insistent the next day that this is where God wanted him and he was not about to leave, and so Nathanael began to canvas around looking for the best place to make a permanent camp where he could easily get water. Where they would get food was another question, but he supposed he would leave that up to John until the point that they were about to starve to death.

John went back to the river and before long was calling the travelers to come to him to be baptized. It took some doing but before noon time, he had another line reaching to the shore and beyond asking to be baptized so that they too would be ready for the Messiah. Nathanael wondered about that too as he walked along the river searching out a place to protect them from the forthcoming winter. Who was this messiah that John continued to talk about so intensely now and would he really save the world from the Roman's, he wondered? He couldn't even imagine the world without Romans. They had been here for as long as he had been around and with his parents before that and their parents before them. And they did it with just a hand full of soldiers that stayed mostly in Jerusalem.

He returned late in the afternoon with no better place to shelter than where they were now and upon seeing the river nothing had changed. They still lined up, John still called out, and the wind brought with it a slight chill.

Chapter 4 – Nathanael

Over the next two months, John baptized in the River Jordon submerging anyone who came to him no matter what their faith. Nathanael watched day in and day out but never got into the water with John although John often asked him to. "We've so many Nathanael," he said often. "And I am just one man." But Nathanael preferred to stay back in the crowds and listen to what they said about this man who lived in the water. Even those who did not get baptized had much to say about him. Some called him a prophet, others said he was crazy, and still others a holy man. Most, however, called him the baptizer and his reputation was beginning to spread throughout the region far and wide for they now came looking for him and not just by accident as the travelers had.

One morning Nathanael awoke to a noise that sounded familiar but was too far away to recognize. He sat up and looked next to him only to see John's blanket empty. He looked around but didn't see him anywhere. "I wish just once he would rest for a day," he said to himself grabbing the pot of beer to clean out his mouth. Pulling on his outer garment he stretched then wiping the sleep out of his eyes he walked down the hill to the river where he heard John's voice growing louder.

"Repent," Nathanael could hear him saying as he drew nearer, seemingly sounding louder than normal. "You must repent and be cleansed for the kingdom of heaven is near."

"And I ask you again, how is it you know this? And who has given you the authority to do what you are doing?" asked a tall man standing opposite the shore speaking to John as Nathanael finally reached the river bank. The bearded man was dressed in a fine white robe and a black keffiyeh headdress both which were way too costly for anyone to wear in these parts. Two others dressed similarly where next to him but said nothing. Because of their stately manner and dress, most of those who had been waiting for baptism had moved away and gave them plenty of room. This man had that kind of power over people and knew it concluded Nathanael.

He was obviously some sort of official as Nathanael looked him over suspiciously wondering what he was doing here, but none of this seemed to faze John who was standing waist deep in water with his arms crossed and facing squarely at the man. He seemed to be studying his features but then finally spoke. "May I inquire as to who is addressing me?" he asked this time in a calmer voice.

The man stroked his beard as he contemplated whether to answer but when John remained silent he finally gave in. "My name is not important. What is important is who you are and by whose authority do you say such things."

John smiled and moved towards the shore. "You are from the Sanhedrin then?" he asked shrewdly.

The priest nodded. "I have been sent by them, yes."

"Jerusalem has nothing better to do than to send its priest to this wilderness area to spy on me."

The priest acted hurt. "We are not spies. We are only looking for the truth. So again I ask you, who are you and by what authority do you do what you do?"

"He's the baptizer," someone yelled from this side of the river. "He is sent by God."

The man glanced up at the one who yelled but as quickly looked back down at John. "So you have been sent by God to baptize, is that your story?"

Nathanael could tell that John was starting to get worked up by the man's sharp brashness. "I do not deny this," he answered in return. "Have you come to be baptized by me?" he asked.

The man smiled shaking his head back and forth. "No, I came to find out who you are and who gave you this authority."

Someone else yelled out from the crowd. "He is the Messiah."

The priest jerked back from John as if he had been startled, a large grin on his face. "The Messiah?" he asked sarcastically. "You are the Messiah?"

John was now just a few feet away, water dripping from his garments, his eyes fixed intently upon his nemeses. Nathanael noticed that John had changed from his normal clothing and was wearing camel hair tied to his waist by a leather belt. Someone had given the outfit to him after having been baptized. His hair was matted from being wet. Nathanael had never seen him angrier. "No, I am not the Messiah," he said speaking the words distinctly and solemnly.

"Then a prophet maybe," he asked suspiciously. "Some say you are Elijah."

"Then you have been spying on me," he said accusingly. "But no I am not Elijah."

"Well then who are you?" he asked in exasperation. "Tell me so that I can report back to those who have sent me. We are dying to hear the truth about you."

"My name is John and I do what I do through the power of God," he answered raising his voice to a different pitch. He was getting worked up now and Nathanael hoped he wouldn't go too far for these men looked to be dangerous. "I am the voice of one crying out in the wilderness; Make straight the way of the Lord."

His answer seemed to take the priest aback. "But why do you baptize if you are not the Messiah or Elijah?" he asked puzzled.

"I baptize with water," John said. "But there is one among you whom you do not recognize; the one who is coming after me, whose sandal straps I am not worthy to untie."

The priest acted confused throwing out his arms and looking around as if asking others this question. "Is this man whom you speak of with us now? Or do we have to go somewhere else to find him."

John ignored the comment. "He is coming," he said forcefully. "But you will not know him when he does because he is the truth, and you do not know the truth."

"Whose truth?" asked the priest, "Yours?"

"God's truth," John answered with great strength. "The truth God gave to Moses and Elijah and the rest of the prophets. The truth that your kind fails to see because you are blind to it."

The priest looked as if he was about to refute him but then suddenly he just shook his head back and forth as if in disgust. "Well we shall see," he said motioning his men to move on. "But in the mean time I would watch what you say or your words may get you into a lot of trouble."

John did not reply as the men turned and walked down the road towards Jericho. Nathanael had thought that they had at last escaped from the priestly class who kept chasing them out of towns. He had hoped that they would leave them alone out here in the wilderness away from their synagogues and towns. Even so, it appeared not to bother John at all for as soon as they had left he began to shout again. Looking around he noticed although the people had at first scattered, many were now standing in line waiting on him.

And then he heard John scream, "Repent. Repent and give yourself to the Lord."

That night Nathanael questioned John about the priests. "Do you think they will give us any problems?" he asked.

John sat stirring the fire with a stick. His face had aged so much in such a short time causing him to always look gloomy and worn out. He hadn't combed his hair in months or taken off that smelly camel-hair shirt that someone had given him. "I like it," he once told Nathanael after having worn it for a few weeks. "Besides, I wash it daily in the river," he had explained. But Nathanael knew that that had been months ago and it saddened him that he no longer had any interest in grooming himself.

"I'm afraid that they may come back with guards," he added after John had not said anything. "Maybe we ought to move on to someplace else?"

That stirred John and he looked up at Nathanael. "My son you worry too much," he said quietly. "God has put us here for a reason and here is where I will stay. If it is his will that guards come and take us away, then so be it, but I will not bother with those thoughts." He looked around towards the river which was completely blanketed in darkness and said. "Besides, there are too many souls that I have yet to save. No, this is where he wants me, and this is where I will stay."

Nathanael knew when John would not budge and so that ended the conversation. He lay back on his blanket and searching the sky saw thousands of stars. God put everyone one there, he knew from the Psalms so why would he not put John here? That was as good an answer that he could come up with but it didn't relieve his anxiety any. If guards came and John refused they could both find themselves in a prison for a long time and that wasn't where he was looking forward to being.

It was a cold blustery day several weeks later as he sat on a log sharpening a knife that someone had given him when he saw several servants with bags strapped to their backs coming down the road. That was not unusual for this path which crossed the river but what was unusual was how big it was and how well dressed the servants were. Nathanael was curious and so stepped up on a large rock near the road used for journeyers to sit on and rest from the trip while they refreshed themselves. He had seen hundreds of such people and caravans but this was something special. There seemed to be at least fifty porters, each carrying a bag on their back and in the middle of the entourage an elaborate litter carrying someone who was very, very rich.

Nathanael looked to see if John had noticed and to his surprise, he did. In fact, John, totally out of his norm, began to wade towards the shore all the while looking towards the litter. He looked more intense than Nathanael had seen him in months. If John expected a confrontation, then he was going to give it to whoever was behind the curtains.

"Stop," he yelled at the porters causing a commotion in the front. This gave John time to climb the bank and move out in front of the leading men stopping them from advancing any further. "Stop, I say. I must speak to your master."

The porters in the lead suddenly became confused looking back for guidance from whoever was that was leading them. This cause the porter's further back in the column to cram against each other causing, even more, confusion. Then as on cue, a very stout soldier on a beautiful large black horse rode up from the rear holding a golden pointed spear in one hand and exposing a long decorative curved dagger tucked neatly under his belt. He pulled the horse up once past the porters and looked down disdainfully at John. "Who stopped my caravan?" he asked as if he didn't know it was the small wet man in front of him.

Nathanael noted quickly that this man was rich. A beautiful solid gold cape hung over his shoulders for warmth and he wore a highly polished silver helmet that had a piece covering his nose. He was obviously a man of importance Nathanael guessed as he watched the man adjust himself in his ornate decorative leather saddle. His horse was also magnificently adorned with a matching gold blanket over its neck and back giving the soldier a stunning show of authority, but there was no intimidation seen on John's face.

"I am John the baptizer," he said with his usual sense of confidence, "and I would like to speak to her highness if you please."

The man nudged his horse up next to John so that the horses head bumped against his chest causing John to take a step back. The horse was obviously trained well. "Get out of the way or I will cut off your head," he said softly but loud enough for everyone to hear. Nathanael knew he meant business and jumped down from the rock to go pull him away.

"Then cut it off," replied John, a slight smile appearing on his face.

His answer scared Nathanael to death. He froze where he was waiting for John's head to fly off. He was sure that his was the last time he would ever see him alive. "Ha," yelled the man laughing. "You are a brave one indeed. What is it you want so that I can get my servants across this miserable river?"

"I wish to talk to your princess," he said calmly. "And then I will be glad to baptize you and your men."

The man kicked his horse lightly and once more the large animal pushed slightly against John's chest causing him to move back ever closer to the bank edge. "Well, I am growing tired of you, my little man, so we're going to do this one or two ways. You move or I will run you through with this spear." With that, he leaned across the saddle and eased the spear against John's chest pushing the tip ever so slightly against him. "Do you understand?"

Before John could answer a woman's voice shouted out from further back and Nathanael turned to see a woman stepping out of the large carriage and began walking towards the front with an equal scowl on her face and was shouting at the top of her lungs, "Who told you to stop?" she yelled. "Who is this man and what is he doing preventing my servants from crossing the river?"

Her shrieking mortified Nathanael for he had never heard a woman use that tone of voice before. She had been throwing her arms in the air while clambering to the front of the caravan pushing servants to each side as she went. In the meantime, John crossed his arms, smiled and said nothing while the guard on horseback drew his spear away and slumped back in his saddle. It was clear that the woman was in control here and no one would do any harm until she got there.

Finally, she got to the front, passing around the large horse which stood in her way and was now staring down at John. "And who are you," she sneered but with her voice much lower than before. "And what are you doing stopping my caravan? Do you not know who I am?"

"In fact, I do," John said self-assuredly looking defiantly at the woman standing before him. "You are Herodias if I am not mistaking from your banners. And you are also the unlawful wife of King Herod Antipas."

Nathanael almost choked at those words. He could not believe that John had said that. This was probably the most powerful woman in the entire Galilee region and he was accusing her of being an unlawful wife of her husband the king. Even if he weren't really a king he was close enough and every bit as powerful, and here was John throwing mud in her face. Nathanael stepped back away from the porters putting distance between him and them because he knew most certainly that this was going to end very badly for John.

Herodias just stood there, her mouth gaped open wide and unable to say a word, but it was obvious that that wasn't going to last long. "What did you say about me you little toad?" she finally asked him. Nathanael could see the little red veins on her neck bulging as her face contorted into a grotesque shape. He had no idea how John stood unmoved before that outrage.

But it seemed that her intimidation did not affect John in the least. "I said that you are the unlawful wife of our king for he is still married to Phasaelis, the daughter of King Aretas of Nabatea and you are an imposter who was once married to your husband's brother." He said this all calmly as if with a good friend with whom he was having a casual conversation. Meanwhile, Nathanael was hoping he would quit with this dangerous game.

Suddenly the woman swung her hand around catching John completely off guard and hitting him full force on the side of his face. The blow was so hard that it caused him to take a step back which landed him in the river because the horse had already nudged him over to the edge of the bank. He came up out of the water fully wet but held his composure. "And that makes you an adulterer," he added wiping the water from his face. "And a sinner," he added as an afterthought.

She snarled. "And who is it that stands before the wife of your king condemning her of falsities?"

Most men would have been shivering uncontrollably in this freezing water with the blustery cold air hitting his wet body but John had been doing this for so long that he was numb to it. "My name is John," he answered.

She looked him up and down as if he were a mere nothing and then spat towards him. "Well John, I can assure you that you are not long for this world for when my husband finds out about what you have said he will have you pulled apart by horses after he has cut your eyes out."

"Well, at least I shall die in the knowledge that I will soon be with God my lady. But you, you will die and be eaten by worms for eternity for committing adultery and incest with the man you sleep with."

She sneered at him uncontrollably but couldn't land another blow without getting wet herself. "I will have your head on a platter," she yelled vindictively then spun around and almost running into the horse screamed at her entourage to begin moving. "And I give you permission to kill anyone who stands in our way," she yelled walking past them.

Fortunately, John was still in the river and so no longer stood in their way as the porters were now free to file by. Herodias' litter was being carried by eight strong servants who ignored everyone else and concentrated on keeping it level which now had its curtains closed. Nathanael watched as the entire group receded down the road and then faded into the dessert on the other side before looking down at John who was still in the water.

Walking up to him he squatted next to the bank shaking his head. "This time, I think you may have made a powerful enemy," he said woefully. "I hope, but I doubt that she will forget this little interruption of her trip."

John looked at Nathanael smiling slightly, his hair and beard matted from the water. "Sometimes the truth is hard," he said and then moved back to the middle of the river for his next baptism.

"And sometimes the truth may kill you," Nathanael yelled at him but then regretted it as he looked up at the crowd looking at him.

Nathanael was worried. This was not just some priestly high-up that he had gotten under their skin. And there had been many, including a couple of Roman cohorts that had passed through one day and would have killed John save for the fact that they were on an official charge from the new Prefect Pontius Pilate and had no time to mess with him. Even a dozen bandits came through one morning but just laughed at him when John offered to baptize them and take away their sins. After finding out that they had no money or food they laughed again and left.

But this was different. This was demeaning a king's wife to her face and that could get both of them in prison or even worse, dead. Afterward, Nathanael tried his best to convince John to move to another river or even better to another country but John would have none of it. "I will be here when they come. If it is God's will that I am put in prison then so be it. I will do his will," he said dismissing him.

Then John stopped speaking suddenly and looked up at Nathanael and smiled. "Nathanael," he said lovingly, "I don't expect you to go to prison with me. I have been remiss about not thinking about you. You know I have a feeling that we will be visited soon by someone whom will change our lives. It will be someone who will change everyone's lives. Maybe then we will be able to find out what God wants of you."

Chapter 5 - Jesus of Nazareth

Nathanael sat on the rocky bank a few yards from John watching him intently as he continued to do his work baptizing the line of folks that seemingly were always there. Whether called to John from far away by the word of mouth or just happened to be traveling along the road, they moved to an ant trail stretching for as far as one could see. In fact, Nathanael could not remember a day when John had not stayed in the water almost the entire day no matter what the weather. Even a flash flood that brought two feet of water running down the river towards him could not stop his baptizing. He would just stand with one foot on the bank and one in the water and dunk the poor souls in the fast running waters often almost drowning them as he did. If there were travelers who came by and wanted to be baptized, John was there waiting for them, his camel hair shirt and leather belt straddling his thin body as he yelled the words repent over and over throughout the day until his hoarse throat would give out.

Why in the world these people came from all across Judea and Galilee to get washed by this man, he could not comprehend. Most of his day was spent speculating what these people were being called to. The tall ones and the short ones, and those who were obviously poor and the rich, and the sickly, and there were so many of those. It was agonizing to watch them go into the water as one person and then climb out of the river as if they were a new one. He had often thought about doing it himself but there were always others lined up waiting their turn and he hated to break in front of them. And so he watched and speculated and was sometimes brought to tears, but often as not he was just plain bored.

It had been weeks since Herodias had screamed at John and Nathanael was still worried that they had not heard the last of that confrontation. She had been furious at John's words about her illegal marriage and her tirade afterward sent chills up his spine. This would only lead to a great disaster he knew and only time would tell when. You could not cross a queen and expect her to just go away. No, something he knew would come up soon or later.

Nathanael was eating a bowl of venison stew and an apple that someone had given them when he saw a small group come up to the edge of the river standing away from the line but in full view of John. The man leading was average height and wore a frayed long white outer garment that was tied by a worn out rope belt. He was accompanied by half-dozen men and a few women who stood behind the men. They were a band of vagabonds from their looks he thought. But then he noted that they looked like any most other bands of travelers making their way through the countryside. The man in front cast his gaze across the waters to those in line and smiled, and then he focused in on John.

Unexpectedly John stopped after having baptized a young girl and her mother and looked up at the man on the bank. The others who had come with him were quietly watching in anticipation of something about to happen, which attracted Nathanael's attention, for it was unusual for John to break his concentration throughout the day. The two men eyed each other with interest like a couple of fighters about to begin a brawl which led Nathanael to place his bowl on the ground and moved closer to the water's edge just in case John needed help.

"Are you he that who is to come?" asked John uncharacteristically quiet. Nathanael sensed that John was for the first time since he had known him, quite stricken by this man.

The man said nothing but smiled slightly and shook his head as if in agreement. John, who nothing seemed to shake anymore, threw his arms open wide and turning in every direction so that all knew he was speaking to them suddenly exclaimed loudly, "Behold, the Lamb of God, who takes away the sin of the world."

Everyone's eyes darted to the man on the shore holding their breaths in anticipation at the next words that would come, but surprisingly they once again came from John. "He is the one of whom I said, 'A man is coming after me who ranks ahead of me because he existed before me,'"

Seeing a changed man before him Nathanael thought that John was uncharacteristically shaken. Few men could do that to him.

"I did not know him, but the reason why I came baptizing with water was that he might be made known to Israel."

And now it was the man's turn, the one John called the Lamb of God, and everyone's eyes now turned to him including Nathanael who was astounded at these words just spoken. Was this the man John had been speaking about all this time, the one he was not worthy to tie his sandals he wondered? He looked at the man closely but there was nothing on his face or in his eyes that gave him any clues. He looked as if he were a man of low means but so did most other people in this region.

To Nathanael's amazement, the man said nothing but took off his outer garment and entered the water wading out to where John was standing. John was obviously surprised and for the first time ever that he could remember had nothing to say. Instead, the man who now stood before him leaned toward him and spoke softly to John saying something. Nathanael couldn't hear what he had said but he did note a puzzled look on John's face followed but his head shaking back and forth and his lips moving as if in rebuttal. But then he stopped as the man said something else and John's shoulders drooped and his head went up and down several times as if in agreement.

Then it happened. John reached out, took the man in his arms and slid him under the water and as he raised him up Nathanael saw him saying something about being baptized which was usually shouted out loud from the depth of his soul. But instead, the words were said softly at which time the man smiled at John, took his shoulders in his hands and said something back to him. Then he turned and waded through the water back to the bank and left with his companions.

Nathanael watched the men leave then looked back at John who for the first time did nothing. He just stood there as if he were frozen, standing as if a statue in the middle of the flowing water. "Come," said Nathanael wading out to get John and taking him by his shoulders and pulling him towards the shore. "I think you need a rest."

The crowd watched in silence as they walked up the hill to their little camp where he lay John down on his blanket. "Here, I have some stew for you. You haven't eaten in days."

John sat up and took several bites of stew. He then stopped and looked up at the sky as if waiting for something to happen but as far as Nathanael knew, nothing did. Then he spoke, not necessarily to Nathanael but more to the entire world. "I saw the spirit come down on him like a dove from the sky and remain upon him."

The words took Nathanael aback but he didn't say anything. Instead, he just sat quietly to see if he would say anything more. John was in a trance almost, his eyes half-closed, his lips trembling but nothing came out for a while. Then he began again. "I did not know him, but the one who sent me to baptize with water told me that whomever you see the Spirit come down and remain, he is the one who will baptize with the Holy Spirit. Now I have seen and testify that he is the Son of God."

Nathanael wanted to ask him what the Holy Spirit was and how this man, a mere human could be the son of God, but he remained quiet. He just watched John sit there in his trance staring out into the world. After a long time, his eyes shut and head drooped and Nathanael leaned him back onto his blanket and covered him up. It was an unusual day, he surmised, quite unusual.

That night Nathanael kept the fire going to warm his friend and continued to ponder on the day's events. "Who was this man," he asked himself a dozen times. "And how can he be the Son of God?" But there were no answers and so he let sleep finally overtake him and slept late into the morning. When he awoke John was not there and so Nathanael got up as he did every morning and headed down to the river.

John was as always in the water calling out to the people who had come to be baptized in his loud husky voice. This time, Nathanael worked with the crowd, keeping them in line and speaking to those who did not know who John was or what he was doing. "He is baptizing in the living water, washing away your sins," he told this one woman who seemed skeptical at what was going on. "He has been called by God to do this," he continued. "Thousands have come to hear him and be washed of their sins. You too are welcomed if you would like."

The woman looked to be thinking, trying to decide what to do when suddenly Nathanael heard John shout out again, "Behold the Lamb of God," he yelled pointing at the shore and Nathanael immediately turned his head to the crowd behind him and saw what he had been pointing at.

It was the man again. The one that John called the Son of God and he was with a small group as he was yesterday but today Nathanael noticed someone with him that he knew.

"Philip," he shouted but not very loud because he didn't want to take away from John if he were going to say more. Philip looked over at the sound of his name being called and immediately a large smile appeared on his face. He mouthed the name Nathanael and dashed through the crowd over to him. "What in the world are you doing here?" he asked excitedly. "I haven't seen you since we were together in Bethel when we were thrown out of the synagogue."

"And the whole town."

Philip laughed. "Yea, the entire town. I haven't been back since."

"We haven't either," he added still not believing it was his old friend. They had begun following John together but Philip had left after a short while and Nathanael had not seen him since.

"So what have you been doing," he asked slapping his old friend on the shoulder. "I see you are still with John."

"Somehow I have gotten myself really attached to him," explained Nathanael thinking back over the last months. "I've have been helping him so much with his ministry. He's an amazing person but sometimes I think he's a bit crazy."

"Yea, he was when I was with him too," laughed Philip.

"So what are you doing here with that man, whoever he is?" Nathanael asked pointing at the strange man who had approached yesterday and had been baptized by John.

Philip looked startled. "Why that is Jesus. Have you not heard or seen him before?" he asked surprisingly.

"No, I don't think so," Nathanael said looking at the figure on the bank. "Where is he from?"

"From Nazareth," he answered, "but mostly stays in towns and villages around Galilee. You wouldn't believe what I've seen Nathanael. He is a truly holy man. His words are like wisdom and he heals the sick and makes the blind see and the crippled walk."

Nathanael keenly eyed the man who was talking intently to some people near him. He looked like anyone else he thought to himself, so how could he be the Son of God? "Nazareth?" he said almost laughingly, "Can anything good come from Nazareth?"

"Well, you wouldn't be so disbelieving my friend if you could see the things he has done."

Nathanael shook his head. "I'm sorry, I didn't mean to be so disparaging. It's just that this all sounds kind of strange; healing and curing people. Anyway, I didn't see you yesterday when John baptized him."

"Oh, some of us were in Jericho yesterday when he came down here," Philip explained. "Last night when we gathered together he told us that John had baptized him. We asked him why he needed to be baptized and he said he just did, that it was all part of the plan. We get that now and then Nathanael. Sometimes he speaks in riddles and it is confusing. Anyway, we came back with him this morning. He wants us to head back up the river towards Galilee again." Suddenly he stopped and took Nathanael by the shoulders. "Say, why don't you come with us and see for yourself?"

It sounded like something that Nathanael would like to do but he shook his head no. "I've got to make sure it is alright with John first. Someone has to look out after him. But if he agrees maybe I'll come up that way in a few weeks just to see what is going on."

Philip smiled. "I think you will be amazed," he said. "We are, every day."

Before leaving spoke to John for a short while and then left with Jesus and his small group and headed up the river towards

Galilee just as Philip had predicted. It wasn't until they were out of sight that Nathanael turned back towards John. "I think I will talk to him tonight," he said to himself as he began to work the line once more.

That night Nathanael and John sat around their fire eating mushrooms and bread. John had grown thin for he refused to eat meat any longer and his beard was getting gnarly and long. They sat mostly quiet each night but this night Nathanael was anxious. John seemed tired like he did most every day and so Nathanael decided he better talk to him before he had a chance to fall asleep. "I have been hearing a lot about this man called Jesus," he said suddenly.

"Really," said John but Nathanael didn't know if that meant he had also heard of him or had never.

"Some of the people from up in the Galilee region have said that he is a prophet."

"That's what they said of me, remember."

"Yes, but they say that this Jesus heals people and forgives them of their sins."

John was suddenly quiet. This wasn't usual for him and so Nathanael waited for him to say something. He looked tired and melancholic to Nathanael which was now his usual demeanor. "Then he could be the one that I speak about," he finally blurted out.

"The one that is to follow you?" he asked.

"Yes, that could be him. But we will have to be sure."

"I would like to go to Galilee and see him," Nathanael volunteered suddenly. "I would not be gone long."

John smiled. "Yes, that would be good. You go and see this man. Then come back and tell me if he is the one we look for."

Nathanael left the next morning. He was happy in a way that he was leaving. John had changed since they had first met in Bethlehem. Then John wasn't so sure of himself. They had met in a square, John speaking about God and how they, the people needed to get right with God or they would see his wrath. His message sounded so vibrant and exciting. Even then he had a tremendous belief in the fact that God had been calling him to do something, but he was not nearly as outlandish in how he came across.

They had laughed a lot early on, especially after having been thrown out of their first synagogue and later the entire town. It had been a victory of sorts. John was tickled to death to know that he had struck a nerve and that the elders of the city were afraid of his words. "It's because they have so little faith themselves," he explained to Nathanael. "They have no idea who God is. They have for so long been about themselves and how much they can prosper that they have forgotten that God is love and that he especially loves those who are meek and humble and reach out to help those who are less fortunate."

Nathanael had liked that message. It was how he had felt too. He had had a yearning in his heart to seek out God and to live a life searching for goodness and wisdom. But he did not understand this calling thing that John felt. But they had been happy and even though they had gone hungry often they always managed to find someone who would share with them. That was the wonder and awe about his message. He would tell people that they were going to hell if they would not repent and the people would give him food for doing so. But then he began to change and Nathanael had seen him grow into this hermit who lived in the river all day long and who ate little. His fervor was impressive but his message began to blur as he continued to speak of another who was to come after him. In fact, this other person had eventually become his message and repentance had faded to the past so that the people would be prepared for this man who was to come to them.

Well, now he would find out. Was this man whom he sought the one they called Jesus? If it was he wondered how he would act and what he would say. Would he be full of passion as John was or more subdued as he thought someone who came into rule the world would be? Would this Jesus be stately and wealthy he wondered? Would he have an army already or was it too early. Thoughts of King David flashed through his head as he tried to picture what this warrior he sought would look like. Alexander the great as a Jew, he said smiling to himself. That's what they waited for; the new Alexander the Great.

Chapter 6 – Who is the Truth

It took three days for Nathanael to make it to the Sea of Galilee where he learned from a couple of fishermen that a curious man who was spoken of as a healer had recently crossed over to Bethsaida which was on the other side of the Sea. Not having any money to rent a boat Nathanael decided he would walk and so set out along the coastal road passing through Tiberius, Magdala, Gennesaret, and Capernaum. He had grown up as a child in Capernaum and so knew every inch of this territory but even so the trip had taken him a lot longer than he had expected. He was tired and hungry and hadn't eaten for several days; his last piece of dried meat long gone when at last he came to the outskirts of Bethsaida. Hoping to find some place to sleep he noticed a large group of people along the water's edge listening quietly to a voice that was hidden from Nathaniel. Curious and with some hope that this might be the one that Philip was talking about, he headed towards the crowd.

There appeared to be several hundred men and women standing on the seashore as Nathanael walked up behind them. The man they were listening to was in a fishing boat; it's worn nets carefully lay across the bow and the small bleached sail neatly tied to the lowered mast. He stood in the bow as he spoke but Nathanael could barely hear as he was so far back and with so many people whispering to each other he couldn't make out a word. Suddenly there was a movement among the crowd and as Nathanael looked around he noticed that the boat he had been watching was suddenly moving away from the shore manned by at least three men, two of whom were now paddling as hard as they could.

"Pardon me," Nathanael said to a pair of farmers who remained by the sea talking to each other as most of the others had dispersed to other parts. "Who was that man?" he asked breaking into their conversation and pointing out to the boat.

The two turned towards Nathanael. "Why Jesus of Nazareth," one of them answered looking at Nathanael curiously.

"Well, what did he say and why were all these people gathered around listening to him?"

"You must be new to the area," the man said suspiciously. "Everyone who is from around here knows who he is."

"No, I am not from here," he said trying to sound casual about it.

One of the farmers looked out to the sea and then back at Nathanael. "We all come to hear him speak, of course. His words are powerful and new. I have never heard anyone speak like him before."

"Well, what did he say?"

The man looked puzzled. "He speaks of life, I guess. He talks about how to live and how to treat each other. It's amazing when you hear him. He's spellbinding."

"Yea and he can heal people," said the other, his eyes wide and full of excitement, "I've seen him myself. I saw him touch a man who couldn't walk and he told him to get up and the man did. It was amazing. I've never seen this happen before."

Nathanael looked back out over the water to see the boat disappearing across the lake. He didn't quite know how to react to what the man had said and so ignored his words. "Where do you think he's going?" he asked instead.

"I don't know. But I'd say he won't go too far. We've been following him for three days and this is what he does. He makes a stop and then goes out for the evening and then appears back a bit further down the coast and talks again."

Nathanael's stomach growled loudly and the two looked at him. Feeling embarrassed he rubbed his tummy before asking the question that was lingering between them. "Can I bother you for something to eat?" Nathanael asked. "I've been walking a long time to see this man and I haven't had anything to eat in days."

"Sorry fellow but we ran out this morning ourselves. We were hoping to find something before we were forced to turn back."

Nathanael slept on the rocky seashore that evening up against a large rock that kept the sea breeze from blowing on him. He was beginning to regret having left John and the surplus of food that they received from those who had been baptized. Now here he was cold, hungry, tired and unsure of even who this guy was that he was hunting for. "You will know him when you meet him," John had told him. When asked how John just shook his head and repeated his words. "Don't worry, you will know."

The next day Nathanael woke with a sore back and massive hunger pains. He got up, washed his face in the sea and began to walk in the direction that he had seen the boat rowing off into the night before. As he walked he began to see others working their way along the coast until by noon there were hundreds of people moving together. Nathanael suspected that they were looking for the boat but he couldn't be certain. As he walked he heard of them speaking of miracles and of healings of every sort and he was amazed at what he heard.

The crowd moved inward and so did he until they reached a large grassy area where at last he saw the man who had been standing in the boat talking to the crowds as he had the other evening. This time, Nathanael could hear him clearly. "I do not accept human praises," he said speaking to the crowd, his body moving in every direction so that they could hear him.

"Moreover, I know that you do not have the love of God in you." He paused for a moment to let his words sink in. He wasn't healing, he was being critical and yet they listened to him anyway and without one objection.

"I came in the name of my Father, but you do not accept me; yet if another comes in his own name, you will accept him." Again he paused looking at each person in the crowd. Eyes shifted downwards or away as his moved among them. Then he continued. "How can you believe, when you accept praise from one another and do not seek the praise that comes from the only God? Do you think that I will accuse you before the Father; the one who will accuse you is Moses, in whom you have placed your hope."

Nathanael couldn't believe what he was hearing. This man was somehow making himself out as a messenger from God and was accusing the people of not believing in him, and they were taking it. Men and women were sobbing and pulling their hair out as he chastised them for following Moses and not him. Who is this guy to speak this way?

"For if you had believed Moses," he continued, "you would have believed me because he wrote about me. But if you do not believe his writings, how will you believe my words?"

He spoke for hours as the people listened to him no one daring to leave. Then suddenly the man words caught Nathanael by surprise. "But there is another who testifies on my behalf, and I know that the testimony that he gives is true. You sent emissaries to John, and he testified to the truth. But I have testimony greater than

John's. The works that the Father gave me to accomplish, these works that I perform testify on my behalf that the Father has sent me."

Nathanael's head was spinning with a million questions. Now it all fit together. This was the man who had come down to the river and had John baptize him. Nathanael remembered John speaking again and again of a man who was to come who was greater than he and whom he was not worthy to tie his sandals. And he remembered John saying that he saw a dove descend on him like the Holy Spirit. Then if all that was true, this Jesus was that man, the one that had been baptized by him, and now if his words were true, John would fade away and this man was destined to rise.

Later that day Nathanael being worn and tired was sitting under a fig tree eating a few figs to curb some of his hunger. He really didn't like figs but when food was scarce he would eat anything. The words from that morning and other thoughts kept running through his head when suddenly he heard someone yelling at him. "Nathanael," the voice came from over in the crowd which was still thick with people. Nathanael looked around then saw Philip pushing through the bodies and waving with one hand. "It's me," he yelled again disappearing for a moment from behind a large man. Finally, he emerged and came running up to him throwing his arms around Nathanael. "My god it is good to see your face again."

Nathanael smiled broadly slapping his friend on the back. "I have been following this crowd for days but haven't been able to get close at all to your teacher. This is crazy, this throng of humanity. Is it like this all the time?"

Philip laughed. "Well I'm afraid so, sometimes a bit smaller, but always a crowd. "But listen," he explained, "I have something important to tell you. This Jesus is the one that Moses wrote about in the law and the one that the prophets wrote about. Come and I will show you. I assure you that you have never met a man like this before."

Nathanael immediately thought of John. He had seen them both together in the river but had never given Jesus much thought. He had obviously impressed John that day but he wasn't exactly sure why he would have. John had told him what had happened afterward but Nathanael could not understand why John had tried to refuse to have him baptized. After all, there was not a person who John hadn't tried to baptize before including a high priest, bandits, and kings. But John had told him that this man was different. That he would change the world.

And now Nathanael was walking behind Philip to go meet this miracle worker and he had mixed feelings about it. He had been with John for so long and knew that he had been sent from God. He wasn't sure about this man Jesus. Who had ever heard of him he had asked himself? He was from that little nothing of a town Nazareth and everyone knew that anyone of any noteworthiness would come from Jerusalem and not from Galilee. But somehow he had got caught up in his mysteriousness and now he would soon meet him.

Nathanael approached Jesus who was sitting on a rock talking to three other men all of who were sitting around a fire. Jesus looked up as he saw Nathanael coming towards him with Philip and smiled looking as if they were friends. There was a small bowl of apricots on his lap, one which he toyed with his fingers.

Nathanael weakly smiled back not sure to this moment what he would say. The man looked no differently than the rest. His short beard and long hair were similar to many men of his age. He didn't seem to have the insanity that John had but instead was laid back and calm. There was something different about him Nathanael was sure but he couldn't put his finger on it. The man looked like any other man with the exception of his intense stare which was a bit unsettling when his eyes locked on him as they were now.

"Here is a true Israelite," he said proudly to the others before Nathanael had a chance to introduce himself. The words shocked Nathanael and then he added, "There is no duplicity in him." He said this as if they had just seen each other the day before and was recounting a familiar story about him to the others.

Nathanael's face burst into astonishment. "How do you know me?" he asked timidly. "Have we met before?"

Jesus continued to smile and spoke with the same familiar tone. "Before Philip called you, Nathanael, I saw you under a fig tree." His explanation was as if it were an everyday occurrence that he would know where Nathanael was.

Nathanael was stunned. How had this man known that he had rested under a fig tree before Philip had found him? He glanced at Philip who had moved nearer to the fire and he looked at him shrugging his shoulders as if he had no idea. Jesus was staring intently at Nathanael much like John would when something was being said that was important. He wanted to say something but he had no idea what to say. Then he thought of John and what John had said about the Holy Spirit descending on this man after he had been baptized and that he had not been worthy to untie his sandals. Then he knew, or something was telling him that this man was different, that he might be the one from God. And if he were then as John had said, things were going to change.

Finally, he sputtered out, "Rabbi, you are the son of God; you are the King of Israel."

Jesus smiled slightly still staring intently at Nathanael. He stood and looked around at the others then turned back at Nathanael, the full attention of everyone now directed at him. "Do you believe because I told you that I saw you under a fig tree?" he asked his hands stretched out holding them towards heaven. His eyes were so focused that it was nearly impossible to look away. "You will see greater things than this," he said softly pronouncing every word as if it meant everything. Then he gazed up. "I tell you that you will see the sky opened and the angels of God ascending and descending on the Son of Man."

They walked along the coastal road towards Tiberius throughout the day and as they did Jesus walked quietly as if he were meditating on something and then suddenly without warning he began to speak. No one wanted to miss anything he said so the group of men and women who walked with him turned their attention towards him quietly in anticipation of what he would say next. Nathanael was fascinated with his stamina and how much he could talk in a day speaking about every facet of life which all made perfect sense but he had never heard put that way before. Rarely during his days with John did they speak about anything and when he did it was more about what had happened that day and nothing philosophical. But when Jesus spoke, he spoke of loving others, not judging, being merciful, and forgiving.

"You hypocrite, why do you notice the splinter in your brother's eyes," he asked intently looking around at everyone to make sure they were all listening. He walked over to his mother and put an arm around her and kissed her on the head, "but do not perceive the wooden beam in your own?" Then he smiled as he often did right before he explained himself. "Remove the wooden beam from your eye first; then you will see clearly to remove the splinter in your brother's eye."

The words stung Nathanael and he felt as if Jesus had been speaking directly to him for quite often he looked critically at others. Knowing that Jesus was aware of his thoughts and actions were disturbing and for the first time, his eyes moved from the master to his feet in shame. Then glancing around the group he noted many of them doing the same thing.

That night he sat around a warm fire with Philip and a number of other followers who spoke of the things said that day. Jesus had gone ahead of the small party leaving them near the shore by themselves. A number of them asked to go with him but he wanted to be left alone and so told them to stay there together. "He does that often," said Philip. "He likes to go out alone and pray by himself."

They shared what food they had with them and it was the first of anything he had had in several days but it wasn't very much. Philip introduced Nathanael to everyone, some who had been off elsewhere when he had first met Jesus. Simon had been there yesterday with his brother Andrew and a good friend Thomas, all who seemed to be eager to be in this small band. Then he introduced James and another named John and a man who had levied taxes for the Romans named Levi who seemed to be nervous. Lastly, there was a colorful interesting man named Judas, who Nathanael liked immediately and another Simon, another James, a guy named Thaddeus and his friend, another named Judas. And there was also an older woman who was with the group but seldom sat near them and her name was Mary whom Nathanael learned later was Jesus' mother.

"What happened to his father," he asked those who were still awake several hours later. "He died several years ago," answered Andrew.

"We didn't know him," added Simon. "Mary is kind of like our Mother who takes care of us and in return, we watch out for her because Jesus is always going off by himself.

"Yea, we adore her," Andrew added and they all smiled shaking their heads in agreement.

Nathanael answered questions from the disciples about what John had been like and what he had said about Jesus and then they shared stories of things that Jesus had done and said until one by one they all fell asleep under the stars. Nathanael lay confused and dazed at the day he had had and wondering what the morrow would bring. He also wondered what he would tell John for he was certain that he would follow Jesus just as the others had decided to do.

"It's kind of strange," said Andrew shaking his head earlier when he was asked by Nathanael why they had followed him. "When he asked my brother and me to come along we immediately left our boats and followed him. I can't tell you exactly why, but there was an allure about him that pulled us to him."

"Yes," added Simon. He was a big man and when he spoke he bellowed out his words, not to intimidate but that was just how he talked. "And ever since we have seen so many strange and wonderful things happening where ever we go. You will be truly amazed if you follow with us, Nathanael."

"Well, where are we going," he asked Simon since it was he and Andrew who did most of the talking.

They all sat silent for a moment looking at each other with all sorts of different expressions on their faces. "He won't tell us," Simon ventured forward.

"He tells us not to worry about things like that and to just follow him. He keeps telling us that we will one day be fishers of men instead of fish," he said looking around for agreement.

This time, Philip chimed in. "I'm not sure what that all means but we have learned not to second guess him or to ask too many questions. We just try and keep up with him."

The next day they found themselves walking with a large crowd who were making their way inland to a higher land where someone had said the healer was speaking again to a multitude already formed. By the time, they found Jesus it was beginning to get dusk and there were thousands sitting around him listening to his words. They moved closer to the disciples who already were sitting near him and Nathanael, tired from a long days walk, sat down to rest his weary legs. He closed his eyes for what couldn't have been a moment when he was suddenly shaken by Philip.

"Here, take this," he was instructed by Philip as he handed him a basket. To Nathanael's astonishment, it was full of fish and bread. He looked up at Philip. "Where in the world did this come from?" he asked fully surprised at seeing all the food.

"From the master," he said pointing to Jesus. "He just keeps putting his hands into the basket and pulling out fish and bread. He's been doing this for over an hour and all we had when we started was a few loaves of bread and two fish we took from a small boy."

"What," said Nathanael? "That's impossible."

"Well there he is, and there are all the people," he answered. "Everyone is eating and there are thousands of them."

Nathanael took a bite of the bread and smiled as he chewed. "Beats me how he did it," he said whispering so as not to be overheard, then added. "Someone could have brought in a huge boat load of fish this morning and spent all day baking bread. I have never seen the likes of this and never will as long as I live."

Later they sat with Jesus around a large fire and Nathanael asked about the loaves and fish. "They were hungry were they not?" he answered in his typical simplistic manner. "But it is not food that they need you see; it is God. And they will find God through his Son. And all will be satisfied as they were today." He paused for a moment and looked around the circle. "And so will you Nathanael, and you Simon, and the rest of you. You will all soon have the meal which will give you everlasting life."

No one dared asked what that meal would be and so waited for him to speak again. He had been poking the fire with a stick while the silence hung around the camp fire. "You see my brothers; they are like sheep without a shepherd. They need me and I will lead them. And you are the light of the world. You see a city set on a high mountain cannot be hidden. Nor does anyone light a lamp and then place it under a bushel basket. No, it is set on a lampstand, where it gives light to all in the house."

He fell silent for a moment looking into each one's eyes with great intensity. Then he said, "Just so, your light must shine before others, that they may see your good deeds and glorify your heavenly Father."

Again, no one said a word but Nathanael knew what they were all thinking. Like him, they were wondering what he meant by that. "What was this everlasting life he keeps talking about," he asked the next day but got no response, "and what is the meal that will be given to us in order to obtain it?"

Chapter 7 – Herodias

"Dispatch that letter now on your fastest rider and make sure that it is delivered only to my husband," barked Herodias as she fumbled closing the letter and put her wax seal on it. "I want it in his hands by sunset tomorrow." She stood on the terrace of her large palace in Machaerus, where she had just arrived the evening before. A tall palm stood next to the balcony throwing shade on her couch where she had been dictating her letter to her Antipas.

She had been pacing for an hour with an occasional stop to pick something up and sling it across the room. Already strewn across the floor was a clay pot broken into small pieces which once held some beautiful yellow and purple flowers, a silver wine goblet, and a small marble bust of her husband Antipas. She had paused at a bust of her grandfather but thought better than to heave it. Only the head guard of her palace had been present during the barrage and he remained as far away from her as he could.

Now holding the letter, the guard's heart sank for it was miles from Machaerus to Tiberius and at best would take two full days of riding to make the trip. But the look in his queen's eyes was so hateful that he knew not to say a word. Instead, as he bowed he decided that he would have the rider take a second horse along and ride all night changing in the morning and then go all day again.

That was all he could do and as long as Antipas didn't mention when the letter got to him then maybe she would never guess. Otherwise, he would be out of a position and his wife and two children would be homeless before the end of the week.

Herodias was so furious at the words of the baptizer that she would probably have had him drawn and quartered herself if he had been in her grasp. But none-the-less she was confident that he would indeed be drawn and quartered as soon as Antipas arrived. Twice she had witnessed someone being pulled apart by horses and how much pain they had gone through before it was over. It was a ghastly sight but she had not turned away from the punishment of the two thieves. One of the men she had been told had lived with his arms out of their sockets and legs that were torn out of their thighs for two whole days screaming the entire time. This is what she had in mind for John the Baptizer and she relished the thought of listening to him scream throughout the evening. He would never again say those words again to her or anyone else once she got a hold of him.

Now alone, Herodias smiled as she toyed with some nuts in an intricately ordained wooden bowl on the table next to her couch. She loved things like this more than anything and her palace showed it for every room was full of such ornate small objects. Why her husband made her go to stay in that awful Tiberius she would never know. He had designed it, had hired all the servants, had decorated probably with some harlot who knew nothing of decorating and he had done this while she was away and without asking her opinion of anything. But here was different. These were her things and her people and her decorations. She may not have designed the palace itself but she had changed enough things to have made it her own.

The servants here she had handpicked and groomed over the years whereas those in Tiberius had been picked by her husband as a gift and she loathed them. Here in her real home she could relax and prepare for the upcoming birthday party which she planned to be the event of the year. Herodias was pleased to be married to her husband for her former husband who was Antipas' half-brother had died shortly after she had left him. What a pickle that would have been, for the Romans would never have let her rule, in fact, they took the rule away from the Jews altogether and put it in their own hands, first with Valerius Gratus and now with Pontius Pilate. She had suspected that her first husband was falling out of favor when she seduced Antipas into her bed several years ago and then convinced him to steal her from his half-brother. But none of this meant that she was an adulterer or was involved in incest. No, John had crossed the line with those words and he would pay for it.

For now, she would wait until she heard back from Antipas but she knew her power over her husband in bed and would use it to make sure that he did as she pleased. Life with her in a foul mood was not what he wanted and tried always to avoid it. The things she had done to him in the past to get him to capitulate to her whim could fill a manuscript. This time would be no different for this John person meant nothing to him or his province nor would his discreet untimely death draw any attention to Rome. No, this would be a quick chapter in her book and one she relished to bring to an end, and she would do anything to get her way.

"Joanna," Herodias called loudly not bothering to look to see if she was near. She often did this and would become perturbed if the person she wanted was not immediately at her side. The servants, being keen to her outburst, worked out a system whereby they would always have one of the staff at her beck and call who could quickly summon another servant if it was indeed someone else that she wanted. Despite Herodias' quick temper they managed to have someone at her side before she would blow up, but occasionally even that didn't matter as her foul mood would override everything.

"Joanna," she screamed again just as the servant was entering the room. "You are all worthless, everyone one of you. I have no idea why I keep any of you on," she scolded. Joanna was used to her moods but was unnerved anyway. "Pour me a bath but make sure it is hot this time. The last bath I had was tepid at best. I do not want to step into another cold bath, do you understand?"

Joanna shook her head up and down as if she had understood. Never had she poured Herodias anything but a hot bath but still the woman complained that she seemed to always never have one. As she headed to the baths Joanna wondered why her lady was rarely ever satisfied with anything in life even though she had so much. Not a day went by when Herodias wouldn't complain about something.

Antipas frowned when he received the letter the following evening just before setting down to dinner and wondered why she had almost killed the rider getting such a non-urgent message to him so quickly. Before him lay an exquisite meal of gazelle, flatbread and honey, and his favorite; a melody of squash, onions, and leeks, but even so, a hundred miles away his wife was still able to ruin one of his favorite meals. He paid the messenger a handsome stipend from his purse and sent him to the guard's quarters to rest for a few days and get plenty of food. He knew that Herodias was intolerant with others when she felt offended and always went well overboard with her wrath and expectations of how much someone should be punished.

He stabbed a leak with a knife but half way to his mouth he changed his mind and slung it across the room nearly hitting his friend Manaen who was sitting near him at the big table. It was large enough to easily sit twenty-four people but there were only two of them that evening. The two had been alone when the leak went flying. Carelessly he dropped the knife onto the table and again picked up the letter scanning the printed blocks with impatience. Who was this man John, and why did he upset his wife so with this foolish nonsense?

"I tell you Manaen," he said as he threw the letter on the table in a rage. "She will be my downfall, I guarantee you. I don't know why I married that woman. She can't ever be satisfied. I could give her a kingdom and she wouldn't be contented."

His friend and confidant knew better than to agree with any reproach towards Herodias for if it ever got back to her that he had said something against her then it would be his turn to forfeit his head. He reached over and pulled the letter out of the gazelle gravy and laid it gently on the table cleaning the grease off of it. Then as if nothing had happened he poured Antipas another goblet of wine and passed him some onions.

"Is there something that I can help you with sir?" Manaen asked sympathetically. He knew there was nothing but it often helped in soothing his master's emotions.

He stood and began walking around the terrace as he spoke. The rest of the servants had quietly hidden themselves to avoid his wrath. "She ran into a vagrant preaching about God and who knows what in the river Jordon of all places and this man accused Herodias of being an adulterer, because for some reason he says that I am still married to Phasaelis, even though I divorced that whining woman, and that because I was the brother, or more accurately the half-brother of Herod II, that somehow she is committing incest." He said this so quickly that Manaen could barely understand any of it.

"I am sure it is nothing that can't be fixed with a sympathetic and conciliatory response to her letter," he said trying to stay as neutral as he could. Life was so much easier when she was away that he longed for her to throw herself into such a tirade that she would collapse and never come out of it. Often he dreamed of her choking on a piece of meat while everyone watched her squirm until she was blue in the face. "Surely she will calm down after a few days once receiving your letter."

Antipas stormed back over to the table and slammed his fist down on it in a rage. "No, Manaen a letter won't do. I must go to Machaerus or there will be hell to pay. Besides," he said shaking his head in disgust. "There is my birthday party that Herodias is giving me in my honor in a few months which I have no way of ignoring, so I might as well go now and nip this thing in the bud before it boils over."

"Well, I am sure that your highness knows better about these things than I and so I will pledge all my resources in helping you get ready for your trip."

Antipas nodded and took a sip of his wine. "You are the best Manaen. I just hope that she has calmed some by the time I get there. If not I may have to drown her in the cesspool."

They both laughed and Antipas felt better. He sat down and stabbed a piece of the gazelle placing it in his mouth. "You know Manaen," he said while chewing the steak. "I have never had any luck with women. They always seem to want more than I can give them."

Manaen cleared his throat. "A trait I might add that is not limited to Herodias and Phasaelis my Lord. From my limited and brief experience with women, they all seem to have the same peculiarity."

Antipas smiled. Manaen's humor was amusing but didn't help in the least with the problem at hand. He would still have to face Herodias head on and it would not be pretty. "Take a letter Manaen to my wife," he said suddenly. "Tell her that I will pack immediately and head to Machaerus as quickly as possible." He paused and something came to him. "No, tell her instead that I will be there once I have visited this John fellow and see what he has to say for himself. Maybe I can nip this thing in the bud well before I have to see her face to face."

Manaen nodded in agreement. "Excellent idea my Lord. Would you like for me to accompany you on this side adventure?"

Antipas nodded slightly. "Yes, I think you could be helpful if we have any problems. Who knows what a crazy person like this will do when confronted with his evil words. We should take a number of palace guards just in case we run into trouble. It never hurts to be prepared." Antipas paused for a moment while twirling his wine. "Will you make sure that is taken care of Manaen?" he asked.

"How many men do you think will suffice," he asked in return.

Antipas shook his head. "You figure that out Manaen. Just make sure we have enough to get out of trouble if we find ourselves in a mess."

"Yes, my Lord," he answered bowing low. Then after not hearing anything further from Antipas, he slowly backed out of the room.

Antipas hadn't even noticed that Manaen had left. He was searching the skies for an omen but after seeing none he gulped down his wine, wiped his mouth, and then once again tried to concentrate on his table. It didn't take long to fill the plate set before him. The ornate clay earth ware was honed outward so that the gravy would not run off the plate. As he knew it would be the gravy was delicious, as was the meat it sat in. But he just wasn't very hungry and so soon tired of the spread and walked to the wall overlooking the city. Fires were aglow here and there but other than those the city was in relative darkness. Few people could afford the oil lamps that were interspersed throughout his terrace and sleeping quarters which gave the entire upper story a glow of its own.

"Bring me another goblet," he shouted to one of the servants who waited not far from him as he watched the sky with interest. A shooting star would be a good omen, he thought as he yawned into the back of his hand. "I will set out the day after tomorrow," he told himself. "We shall see what this man named John has to say for himself."

Herodias received his letter two days later after Antipas had already left Tiberius. He had timed it so that he would be long gone from the palace before she had a chance to write him another letter demanding something else of him. This infuriated her but there was nothing she could do short of leaving herself to try and intercept him at the river where John was. But that was not very doable as he was just a few days ride from the Jordon whereas she was at least four days. And taking into consideration that he had already left that would surely mean that she would show up well after he had confronted the baptizer.

"I tell you, Joanna," she fumed pacing back and forth near the pool of the atrium the next day. "If he doesn't arrest that man I will never speak to him again." The water was only a foot deep and even though the roof was open above with a large hole in the ceiling it had not rained in so long that the servants were filling the pool using large clay pitchers. The old dusty water had been emptied first and then the ornate tile figure of a dolphin had been scrubbed and made to shine again. Herodias had supervised the entire operation and was glad that she had because they would have never scrubbed the tile she was sure. Joanna was a personal servant that did almost anything that Herodias needed throughout the palace but she was still a servant and prone to cutting corners if not watched. It was an important position that went to her because she was the wife of their favorite steward, who along with other duties, made sure the stores in the house was full of the finest meats, vegetables, wines, fruits, and nuts. He was indispensable, and therefore his wife was treated well.

After inspecting the pool Herodias turned to head back to her living quarters. "Make sure this is finished, Joanna. I shall take a rest now," she said before she was half-way through the door. "And make sure that I am not disturbed. It infuriates me when you disturb my naps," she yelled from the outer hallway.

Joanna said nothing. Never in her tenure at the palace had Joanna ever disturbed Herodias during her nap. Like everything else, she blamed her waking too soon on her servants but never on herself. She waited for a few moments before taking leave of herself and heading off in the other direction. "Make sure the water is completely full and that there isn't any on the tiles," she explained to the two girls who continued to pour the water. "I shall be in the kitchen if you need me."

The large kitchen palace was separate as were most kitchens in large homes due to fire but was connected by a substantial walkway between it and the great house. It was also a refuge from Herodias whom seldom ventured into that part of the palace. Joanna knew the lady well and knew that she was very lazy but also very opinionated. She complained about everything and about everybody and would never listen to others no matter how good a point or idea that it was. And just as often as not she would come back later and use the same argument that she had discredited earlier, and thereby change her original instructions.

Herodias she knew was spoiled, rude, and generally, a tyrant who could care less about the people who worked for her. She was always scolding, never polite, wasteful, and just down right mean all the time. Nor was she satisfied with her husband Antipas who tried his best to appease her but failed miserably as did everyone else except for her daughter, Salome.

Salome, like her mother, was quite striking but unlike her mother who had grown older, she was still maturing as a youthful woman preparing to marry. At fifteen she was already past marriage age but had been promised to Philip who was visiting Rome and would not be back for some time. Herodias doted on her daughter giving her anything that riches could buy providing that she did everything that her mother told her to do. This often infuriated Antipas, her stepfather, who wanted the girl to be more independent and far less dependent on her mother. But as with everything else, Antipas never won that battle and Salome succumbed to her mother's will.

It was Salome whom Herodias found bathing in the pool near the bedrooms as she went for her nap. "Go away," Herodias said to the servant who had been helping her daughter with the bath. "I will talk to my daughter in private."

The servant girl left immediately, knowing of Herodias' wrath to those who dallied around and did not jump when she spoke. The decorative tile walls of the room were wet with moisture from the heat of the bath. "I do wish they would learn to heat my bath correctly," said Herodias as she sat down on the edge of the pool and ran her fingers through the water.

"Oh mother," said Salome dismissing her mother's whining. "Your baths are always perfect. Who would not do exactly as you order and expect to keep their heads?"

"Well that's not why I am here my dear," she said changing the subject. "We have to plan your father's birthday coming up in a few months and I need your help especially with the entertainment." She paused looking around the room as if it were for the first time. Then unexpectedly she turned her gaze back to her daughter. "What do you think we should do?"

Salome frowned. She hated when her mother tried to get her involved with things like this. She almost never took any of her suggestions and if she did it would become her own within the day. She was a whirlwind when it came to planning parties and no one dared get in her way. Even the servants laid low when she began to plan. "I have no earthly idea," she said sounding exasperated. "You decide mother."

Herodias was up and began pacing as she always did when planning. "We shall plan for an enormous dinner for starts," she said as if she could see them all laid out before her. "Nothing will be spared. The best wines mind you, and none of those horrible jars of that stuff he makes in Sepphoris. And of course, the best lamb but

110

none of that tasteless gazelle meat that he loves so much and I can't stand."

She paused for a moment and gave Salome a chance to jump in. "But mother," she blurted out before Herodias had a chance to begin again. "Isn't this his birthday? I would think we would serve what he likes?"

Herodias laughed. "It is his birthday in name only, my dear. It is only an excuse to throw the party of the year. We will invite everyone who is anyone. Even that horrible Roman Pilate should come. And just to make things interesting I will invite his half-brother Philip from Iturea."

"But mother, he's such an awful man," she exclaimed raising herself slightly out of the water as if that would stop her mother from doing something stupid.

"Yes isn't he," she answered laughing. "But he is a relative and it would show unification to Pilate. Yes, I think he will be fine even if he does drink too much. And of course we shall invite every important figure from Machaerus and I guess from Tiberius as well, even though I hate that awful man Manaen who is always trying to usurp me with my husband."

"Well that at least will make papa happy," Salome said sarcastically rising up out of the water. "Hand me a cloth will you please mother and my robe."

Herodias did so and was envious of her daughter's youth as she watched her dry off and put on her robe. "You will make your Philip a wonderful bride my dear," she said thinking back on her youth. "By the way, will he be back in time for the birthday?" she asked.

"I am not sure," she answered sadly. "His last letter said that emperor Tiberius was still out of Rome and won't be back for another month. He can't come home until he sees him."

"Well, then you will have to come alone. I will have a new gown sewn for you to show off your beautiful figure. That will make all the women jealous."

Salome shook her head. Her mother was so shallow when it came to things like that but there was no use arguing the point. "Thank you mother," she answered politely trying to not sound too unimpressed. "Now if you don't mind I must go get dressed for dinner. We have ample time to decide on the guest list."

"Oh no, we don't my dear," barked Herodias at her daughter stopping her at the door to the outside hallway. "I will not take the chance of having someone not be here because they didn't get the invitation early enough. I will come up with a list myself and then you can review it."

"But mother, I don't know any of these people and surely do not care who comes so it would be just a waste of time to look at your list."

Herodias held her tongue as she did not want to get into a shouting match with her daughter. "Well you will look at the list because this is your father's birthday and you should be involved." She pause for a moment hoping Salome would say something but when nothing was forthcoming she continued on. "Now please help out," she asked nicely despite the frown on her daughter's face. "I will have it finished for you before the end of the day. Now off with you and I will see you at dinner."

Salome frowned again but said nothing as she turned to leave. She decided to stay with a friend that night so that she wouldn't have to look at the dreadful list.

Chapter 8 – The Messiah

Jesus never seemed to stop. He was as bad as John for getting up in the mornings before everyone else and taking off on his own or getting into an intense discussion with a stranger. Each day as they began to move they inevitably would run into someone that needed to be attended to or healed, and he would do it. If there were a hand full of people he would stop to preach, and if not, they would then move on to the next town wherever that may be. There was not a day or a moment that went by where Nathanael was not amazed at what Jesus said or did.

"I still can't believe that he made the man walk," he whispered to Philip as they walked along together following Jesus and many others who had tagged along to see what he would do next. They had just left Chorazin where Jesus had healed many and were heading back to the Galilee area. Nathanael wiped some dust from his eye with his fist and coughed from the dust hanging along the road made from a hundred goats that were being led down the road. "But what good did it do?" he asked. "He was a crippled beggar and now he's a walking one."

"Yes, but the man got his life back," explained Philip in a low voice so that no one would overhear them. "Don't you understand that?" he asked.

"Well, I guess so," replied Nathanael confused as he often was with Jesus.

Jesus did a lot of unexpected things and mostly he did so without explanation, although the day before Jesus had told them a strange story about someone sowing seeds and how some of the seeds fell on a path and were trampled while some fell on rocky ground and wouldn't grow and some fell in a thorn patch and were choked to death. Then Jesus sitting around a fire explained the story as if he were explaining how the world was created. But at the end Nathanael still wasn't sure why he had told the story in the first place nor was he sure any of the rest of the twelve knew either. He was such a confusing man.

"Why does he do that?" he asked later that day when Jesus asked to be alone for a while and had walked off from them a distance away. "Why does he not tell us plainly what he's talking about instead of using these parables and short little declarations?" They were all sitting on the dirt as there were no rocks or logs in that area. The sun was hot and the air dusty. James passed around a wineskin and some dried meat. Peter was playing poking at a scorpion with a stick that had been scurrying across the sand looking for prey.

"Because he wants you to remember it, that's why " Peter explained as he rolled the scorpion over onto its back. "Would you have remembered the story about how we grow in our faith if he hadn't explained it with the seeds falling everywhere? You see, we all remember that story don't we?"

"Yea, and the one about the fig fruit and how you don't get good fruit from bad bushes," added James.

"Or was that a vine?" asked Andrew.

James shook his head. "Not sure but it had something to do with good fruit."

"And don't forget," added Peter, "the woman who wiped his feet with her hair and he somehow explained it with the people who were in debt with their master."

"Yea, that the one who has the larger debt has the most to be thankful for," Andrew finished.

Nathanael understood them but what he couldn't understand is why he just couldn't be plainer when he spoke. "I just wish he would be clearer," he said but no one was listening because Jesus was seen walking back down the road to them.

He reached them and sat down among them as if he wanted to say something but wasn't sure how to go about it. Everyone knew this sign. They could tell when it was time to listen up because something was going to be said and that it was sure to be significant. He did his thing about looking at each one intently before he started.

"I've been thinking of you," he began. "My father has entrusted you to my care and yet I feel that sometimes you don't know me." He looked around and everyone seemed flabbergasted, especially Peter who was about to speak up but Jesus held out his hand as to prevent him.

"Then tell me," he said looking around at each one of them again. "Who do they say that I am?"

Nathanael looked towards Peter, as did everyone else but he wasn't the first to speak. Judas instead spoke. "They say that you are Elijah," he offered.

"And I've heard some say that you are John the Baptist," said Andrew.

"And I heard someone say you were one of the prophets of old," declared Philip. Nathanael wanted to say something but he really didn't have any idea what people were saying about Jesus or who he was.

Jesus nodded and looked at the ground before speaking again. He looked tired to Nathanael. "But who do you say that I am," he asked sounding somewhat uncomfortably, his face now turned intently at his Apostles.

No one said a word for a moment then Peter finally spoke up. "Why Lord," he said. "You are the Messiah of God."

Nathanael was sure that Peter had said the right words but Jesus did not smile and shake his head up and down as if he had been correct. Instead, he lifted his head towards the sky and said, "Tell no one about this for it is not yet my time."

Then he stood and looked around at the small group. They were about to get more Nathanael was sure but he had no idea what he was about to say. "Whoever wishes to come after me must deny himself, take up his cross, and follow me." He paused for a moment but no one dared say a word. "For whoever wishes to save his life will lose it, but whoever loses his life for my sake and that of the gospel will save it."

Nathanael held on to every word and even though they didn't make sense he felt something powerful being told here. That he would one day be required to give up his life for this man if he wished to follow him was clear. He felt a chill run down his back although there was nothing but heat bearing down upon him from the sun. But of all things that disturbed him it was his heart beating furiously against his chest.

"What profit is there for one to gain the whole world and forfeit his life?" Jesus continued asking the question without expecting an answer. "What could one give in exchange for his life?" He paused looking and searching as if he knew each one's thoughts. "I tell you," he finally said, "whoever is ashamed of me and of my words in this faithless and sinful generation, the Son of

118

Man will be ashamed of when he comes in his Father's glory with the holy angels."

No one said a word, they all just stared at him each trying to understand in their own way why he had been speaking to them specifically. Nathanael especially was concerned that this had been for him for how often had he questioned what Jesus had said or why he had said it. He felt sweat beading upon his brow but was too ashamed to try and wipe it off. Then a tear welled up in his eye and he did everything he could to hold back the tears. He had let him down this day but swore to himself that he would never do so again.

"I feel my Father calling me Peter," Jesus said that evening after having laid out his bedroll. It was a solemn statement that immediately drew everyone's attention. "I would like it if you would accompany me to the mountain tomorrow." All eyes moved towards Peter who said nothing but you could see the expression of pride on his face at being called out. Then he laid his head back down and as if an afterthought, "James and John, you might want to be with us also."

The next day the nine stayed behind below the mountain as Jesus, with Peter, James and John climbed the steep path that led to the top of the mountain. Nathanael, after promising himself never to question Jesus again did just that. "Why don't you suppose that he didn't take us all with him," he asked the others as they eat some bread and honey for their noon time meal. "What did James and John do that would warrant them to go and not us?"

"Oh, Nathanael, be quiet," said Andrew. "You are always second guessing everything. Don't you know by now that our Lord does certain things in certain ways and rarely does he tell us anything before he does it?"

Nathanael knew that Andrew was right. There was no reason for him to try and question Jesus and what he did. He would tell them in due time or he might not tell them at all but it was not his place to question it. He shut up and watched the trail up the mountain as if to see them still climbing but he couldn't.

Later that day Nathanael was napping when he felt a nudge in his back. "They are coming back down," said Philip.

"Where," asked Nathanael jumping to his feet his eyes directed at the mountain trail.

"There, no up. Yes, up there. Do you see them?"

Nathanael looked further up and immediately saw the three men climbing down the steep trail but they were still some ways away. "It will take them at least another hour to get here," he said disappointedly.

An hour later the four came into camp and Jesus motioned for all of them to come and gather close. Nathanael was sure that he would now tell them what that was all about but once they all gathered around Jesus told them that they would be leaving this spot and moving back towards Bethsaida the next day. "There are so many people that need us," he explained. "We must move on so that they too can see the Son of Man and be healed."

That night the air was cool and clear. Nathanael remembered the days on the river like this and once again thought of John and wondered how he was doing. He remembered the many months he watched him standing in the water calling to those who came by and dunking those who listened to his call. In a way, he missed those days for they were exciting and John did little to keep him off guard like Jesus always seemed to be doing. The followers of Jesus were never sure of what was going on, where they were going, or why he did some of the things that he did. All they seemed to do was to follow him, watch what he did, and then listen to him when he had something to say. It seemed to never end.

The next day seemed to be like all the rest as they followed the healer along the road that would lead them to the Sea of Galilee and over to Bethsaida. But that night Nathanael heard for the first time something that frightened him. Jesus, sitting around the fire had been eating but suddenly stopped and looked among his followers. Then he said most unexpectedly, "The Son of Man is to be handed over to men and they will kill him, and three days after his death he will rise." Then he excused himself and said he needed to pray. Peter offered to go with him but he refused him. "No, Peter," he said sadly. "I need to be alone with my Father."

Nathanael wanted to ask the others if they knew what in the world he had been talking about with dying and rising but was

121

beaten by James. "What did that mean?" he asked looking to everyone. "He will be killed and then rise?"

None one said a word for they were all thinking heavily as to what those words had meant. "Shall we ask him," asked Philip after no one had said anything for some time.

Peter shrugged his broad shoulders. "I'm not sure my friend what he was trying to tell us. But if it were urgent or important surely he would have given us more."

Several heads motioned that they agreed with him. "Maybe we should just wait and see if he explains himself further," he added. "If not, then we can bring it up in a few days."

Nathanael could not get the words out of his head, nor did it seem that the others could either for there were whispers until late in the night about what he had said. Why in the world did he tell them that and then just go off, Nathanael wondered as he looked out at the night sky. He felt depressed and alone even with the others so near. What was all this talk about dying and who would want to kill him?

Several days later, Jesus gathered the twelve together and spoke to them by themselves. Nathanael listened intently as he heard Jesus tell them that he wanted them to go out in groups of two's to the countryside and preach the gospel and expel demons. Nathanael couldn't believe that he was being asked to do just what John had done for over a year or more when he was with him. After saying this they all glanced at each other wondering how he expected them to do this, but Jesus assured them that he had given them the power to do so and not to fret and for them to have faith.

So Nathanael and Philp went together walking across the countryside speaking to anyone who would listen and tell them about Jesus. To their surprise, many had already heard about the healer, as he was commonly called. More often than not someone would tell them the story of a friend or loved one who had gone off to see Jesus after he had come to a nearby town and they had come back a whole person. The two listened intently to all the stories shaking their heads enthusiastically and then eagerly telling them that this Jesus was the messiah and that he had come to set them free.

"But free from who," asked a man who was weeding his wheat on a long winding hill. "Is Jesus going to stop the Roman's from collecting taxes that are killing us?" he asked.

As they returned they were retelling their experiences and to Nathanael's amazement everyone one of them had heard the same thing. "No one wanted to hear about God," he said to the group. "They wanted to be free from their taxes."

They were all seated around a warm fire sharing their stories but instead of Jesus sitting and talking like one of them, Jesus was standing and listening and watching them intently discuss their experiences. Most of the twelve echoed the same sentiments. The people were demoralized and wanted to be freed from the shackles of the Romans.

"And what did they say about me?" he asked. "Who do they say that I am?"

"A great healer," said James after a long pause and they all nodded in agreement.

"The Messiah was to come from the stem of Jesse and King David," said Judas vindictively. "The Messiah will not come from Nazareth. He will not be some lowly preacher and part-time healer but will be a powerful leader and will set us all free from the heel of the dreaded Romans."

Everyone stared at Judas. And as he did typically when he did say something, he turned to walk off. Nathanael watched him with repugnance as he had been getting worse about his critiques of Jesus as time went on and he had been spending more time alone than with them.

"And how true that wisdom is Judas," Jesus said loudly before Judas had taken too many steps. "The Messiah will not come from Nazareth as is explained by the prophets. He will come from Bethlehem, the city of David. Yes, how true your words are."

Judas half-turned as if he was going to say something but then decided not to and walked away. "Poor Judas," Jesus added looking around at the group. "He has so much to understand and yet he rarely ever listens."

He then paused for a moment gathering his thoughts as he often did. He was watching Judas continue to walk away and Nathanael thought that he looked sad. Why would Jesus feel anything about that money grubbing zealot he wondered. Judas was in for himself and no one else, and he and all the rest were growing tired of his lousy moods. He watched as a dust swirl spun a few feet behind Judas causing him to duck his head in his arm and jog away.

They were all quiet as Jesus waited patiently until Peter finally spoke up. "Master, something happened to Andrew and me that we would like for you to explain."

Jesus nodded and waited while Peter got his nerve. "We had been walking all day and had stopped by a well at the edge of a small village and had begun speaking about you to a couple of men who had been watering their goats when a crippled man who had overheard us approached the well. I noticed that one of his feet was twisted so much that he could barely walk. Andrew was doing most of the talking when this crippler came up to me and asked me to heal him."

Jesus smiled. It was that fatherly smile that he often gave them when they were mystified at something that he did or said. "And what did you do Peter," he asked him.

Peter looked astounded. "I reached out to him and touched his shoulder, and when I did I felt something rush through my arm onto him. I had never felt this sensation before."

Jesus said nothing but nodded as if he knew what he was about to say. Peter glanced around as if he were wondering if anyone there would believe him. "Well," he muttered, "then the man took my hand and kissed it and he thanked me and then turned and walked off." Peter took a deep breath, pausing briefly and then finally as if he wanted to get it over with he said almost shouting, "And he was walking steadily as if there was nothing wrong with his foot."

Jesus stood and walked over to Peter and gave him a hug. It was something that he didn't do very often but when he did it was always dramatic. Nathanael saw Peter crying on his Lord's shoulder and tears began to fill his eyes also. Then he whispered something into Peter's ear and went back to sit down.

"Did anyone else experience something like Peter did?" he asked as he looked around at them. Suddenly hands began to rise and before long every hand was raised. "Did I not tell you that I would give you the power to be there in place of me?" he asked as if he wasn't sure why they didn't believe him. "You will see much greater things than these I can assure you."

They spoke among themselves that evening after Jesus had asked that they excuse him and then walked into the hills alone.

Nathanael finally spoke after hearing many of them tell their stories about healing. "A blind man was sitting on the ground begging with a cup in his hand when Phillip and I came by him. His young son was next to him and shouted out to us to heal his father. I told him that we were there not to heal but to share the good news of the messiah with them." Nathanael's eyes again teared up as he looked at Peter. "Then the boy said, 'I saw your teacher heal others, why can't you heal my father.'"

Nathanael could say no more as the tears began to stream down his face so Philip who also was crying but not as deeply spoke up. "So Nathanael reached down and lightly touched the man on the head, and suddenly he was up on his feet shouting and spinning and grabbing everyone he could find." Philip too was having a hard time saying the words and so Nathanael finished. "Because he could see."

Chapter 9 - Machaerus

Antipas heard John yelling well before he actually saw him. He had been riding close to the rear all morning long with a terrible headache until suddenly the procession stopped dead. That is when he heard the voice. It was loud and sounded hoarse but was full of spirit and determination. He smiled at himself as he climbed out of his saddle anticipating the confrontation. As he began to walk past the bearers and mules he surprisingly noted that his headache had suddenly disappeared. "Well at least I owe him that much," he said quietly to himself.

He had worn his military dress so that he would look more commanding upon their meeting. He had learned a long time ago when he was just starting to rule that authority was everything and that whoever could show off the most usually won the day. This day he had a shining silver chest plate draped with a gold cape with an embroidered red letter 'H' on it that represented the line of Herod. His white tunic, made of pure linen, covered his entire body beneath the armor from his neck to his feet, with embroidered sleeves reaching to his wrists. He fingered the hilt of his silver short sword that had been given to him by his grandfather when he had become king of Galilee and Perea. If this didn't intimidate this man then nothing would.

Antipas walked all the way to the edge of the water without saying a word. He had faced many an antagonist while ruling his thirty years and knew much about setting the stage before ever the negotiations got started. He looked down in the water and frowned, for standing before him was a terribly thin man, his long filthy hair matted and tied together with a rope stretching down to his lower back. The emaciated face was dirty as was a horrible camel-hair coat he wore half opened showing his belly and hairy chest. Why in the world would his wife even talk to such a country-dweller, much less listen to his words he wondered in amazement? This pitiful excuse of a human didn't even deserve a comment much less a debate over something serious such as his bloodline.

Antipas looked around noticing for the first time the dozens of people lined up on the other shore waiting to get out into the river. Tall reeds lined the shore casting a shadow on that side of the river and several bodies eased their way into the thickness so as not to be seen. One woman who had already been dunked was standing near the baptizer, her hair still dripping upon her wet robe, her eyes cast down sheepishly at the water as was everyone else's. The water flowed easily around her robe as she stood shivering and afraid to move. Behind her a man and his son stood waist deep, their eyes looking down at the water also so as not to draw attention although both were tall and stood out among the others. Some of the faces looked homely and poor but some also gave the appearance of people who may have possessions. A fine fur cloak or unpatched robe gave them away as being of some substance. He wondered what they saw in this man and what would draw them to him. Whatever it was, it certainly did not concern him nor should it have concerned Herodias. She should have just rode by keeping her curtain closed and let the man yell to his heart content, which was exactly what he was going to do. Abruptly and without acknowledging the man at all, he turned to go back to his horse. Herodias would just have to live with it.

"Your highness, Herod Antipas," shouted John in his typical confident voice, his words echoing throughout the shallow valley as they always did. The next words were softer but just as powerful. "Thank you for coming to see me."

Antipas stopped in his tracks. There was nothing that could possibly come from speaking to this creature, but there was something about his voice that captured his attention and made him spin around and face the man. "What an odd remark," he said casually, his eyes fixed on the pitiful man in the water while moving his fingers back to his sword hilt. He had always been cautious even when the situation seemed innocent enough.

John smiled. "Not really," he replied his eyes wide in anticipation of their meeting. "I was certain you would come. You see the words that I spoke to your wife were meant for you and not for her. I could care less what she thinks. I said them so that you would come, and here you are."

This caught Antipas completely off guard. The man seemed to be much more educated than he had first appeared to be. His first thoughts were that this man was a mute or even an idiot and would have little to say. Instead, he came across quite cultured and educated. There was something about him that perked Antipas' interest and he was curious to find out more from him.

"And who do you think you are summoning me to?" he asked softly but in a commanding voice that knew power. His eyes fixed intently on the man in the water.

"Why I am your conscience," he said equally as soft and commanding, pausing to let his words sink in. "I am here to lay your sins out for the world to see. Then I will cleanse them in this water as you repent them."

Antipas smirked, his lips curling inward as if he had just tasted something he hated. "And what sins may that be," he asked guardedly. It would not do to allow this man to spout out too much in front of his servants but he was now interested as to what this man thought he knew.

"Your marriage, of course," John answered as if everyone knew about it.

Antipas chuckled as if he had something funny. There was nothing that this man could tell him about Herodias that he didn't know but for some unknown bizarre reason he wanted to hear anyway. "And what may that be?" he coolly asked.

John raised his hand pointing a finger at Antipas. "You married your brother's wife," he said accusingly. "And unless you repent you shall rot with her in eternity where the worm does not die and the fire is not quenched."

This time, Antipas laughed loudly. "So?" he asked finally. "He was a worthless husband and now he is dead. Who cares?"

"God cares," shouted John back at him his face cringing with disgust and his finger now pointing towards heaven. "And he will make sure you pay your retribution."

That struck Antipas hard. He had married Herodias after she had left his half-brother and they had been divorced. She might have been a spoiled brat but she had hated her husband and he had treated her badly. Why would this preacher care about that he wondered as his mind raced back to those days when he had seduced her into his bed? She had come willing and then had asked for a divorce. And there was nothing more.

"Why should God care about such an insignificant thing as this?" he asked his voice now showing some concern. "Many people get divorced. Moses himself gave a decree that his people could obtain divorces."

"Insignificant," yelled John. "Insignificant," he shouted again. "Are you blind? Herodias is your half-sister and yet you married her even while she was still married to your brother."

Antipas now on the defensive had no idea how he had gotten there. "She was divorced when we got married," he spat out trying to sound credible.

"Not in God's eyes. You married your brother's wife who was also your half-sister by birth and unless you repent of this you will pay dearly."

Antipas stood dumbfounded. No one had ever spoken to him this way much less had ever accused him of such atrocities. His eyes darted around the crowd looking to see if anyone was agreeing with this man, but of course, every head was bowed low as if they had not heard a word. It was then that Antipas realized his mouth was ajar and he quickly closed it. Then he looked toward his friend Manaen who was standing a few feet to his side and who had so far not said a word. He hoped for some sort of support from him but found none. Only the rustling of leaves from a stiff breeze broke the silence of the river bed and Antipas began to sweat.

John remained silent for what seemed an eternity. He knew he had struck a nerve and now waited to see if the great man standing before him would confess that he had sinned. For most of the exchange their eyes had been locked on one another but now Antipas' eyes were darting here and there searching for allies only to find none. It was strange that someone as powerful as he seemed so pitifully pathetic at the moment. If he had been a rodent he would have scurried into a hole by now.

Antipas had to do something. He took a deep breath to help gain control of his emotions and refocused on the man in the water. The cool breeze sweeping down the river helped settle Antipas down some and gave him a moment to think. Nothing he said could displace the words that the baptizer had said for to some extent what he had said was true. It was the fact that he had said them which disturbed him for up until now no one in their right mind would ever have brought it up. And now these words settled on him like a heavy weight on his shoulders, the air thick with anticipation as to what was going to happen next.

"Manaen," he said firmly nodding at his friend. "Ask Publius to come forward."

John said nothing but watched as the first man disappeared into the throng and then returned a moment later with a soldier that from the way he was dressed quite obviously carried an important rank. The man came forth and bowed to Antipas. "My Lord," he said his eyes darting towards John.

"Publius," Antipas said no longer paying any attention to John but none the less was pointing at him in the water. "Arrest this man and bring him along with us." As he was about to turn away he suddenly stopped and looked back at Publius. "And flog him a dozen times and then make doubly sure that he is tied securely to the mule so that he can't escape. And if he says a word shove some of the donkey's dung in his mouth."

The whipping was brutal. It was the first time that he had ever experienced it. They had removed his shirt and tied him to a tree so that he couldn't move and then one of the guards pulled out a whip which had little barbs attached to the end and flogged him twelve times. The barbs caught in his back and pulled his skin off as they came free. Blood had run down his pants legs and onto his bare feet. Nothing had ever hurt as bad.

John said nothing for his back stung and besides it wasn't to the guards he wished to talk to, it was Antipas, and he was well away from him in front of the procession riding his horse. The walk was strenuous after all those months just standing in the water but he kept to his feet and spoke nothing. Flies kept hovering around his back but the camel hair shirt helped keep them off his wounds. It took four grueling days to cross the desert plains and mountains of Perea resting each evening near a river or stream until well after the sun had risen on the next day. The guards shared their food with him but none spoke for fear that he might somehow implicate them also.

The first night he was unable to rest on his back and so was forced to sleep on his stomach. They gave him no blanket and tied his hands to a tree so that he could not roll over even if he had wanted to. Antipas paid him no mind and so John remained quiet throughout the day except for on occasion when he asked for water. The sun beat down on his arms and forehead making them red in the evening and his feet, which had no sandals on them, became bloody as well. He began to weary and hoped that it wouldn't be long until they came to their destination.

Around noon on the fourth day, the procession rounded a ridge and John saw for the first time the city of Machaerus. The white limestone buildings reflecting light from the sun caused the city to sparkle on the hilltop. It was very large with numerous ramparts set around the walls and two immense castles on either side of the valley for protection. The road they were on slowly curved down the hill making its way towards a large gatehouse which stood forty feet high and as equally wide. Only Jerusalem itself was larger and grander.

They had stopped just inside the gate where John watched Antipas turn his horse over to a stable boy before walking briskly over to him. "Publius," he said hurriedly taking the soldier by his coat and pulling him towards John. "Take the prisoner to my cellar and shackle him to the wall. You may feed him and give him water but do not let anyone talk to him or take him anywhere. Not even Herodias, is that understood?"

Publius muttered something in agreement and bowed then grabbed John by the neck of his coat and led him away. The streets were dusty and full of children and an occasional dog that barked as they walked by. They passed a tall stone synagogue where doves sat resting on the overhang of the entrance way and a Jew with a long beard and high top hat watched them go by. Few of the inhabitants paid any attention to them for everyone was busy carrying wares or pushing carts to and fro. Only the two guards with long pointed spears standing on either side of the castle entrance acknowledged their existence but said nothing.

The main hall of the castle was cool even as hot as it was outside. The tile floors echoed as they walked to the far side of the keep and entered through a large wooden door that brought them into another chamber with a throne on a dais on one side and chairs on the other. Several large tapestries hung on the opposite walls which soften the sound of the guard's boots. One other smaller door stood near the dais and one of the guards stopped to open it. Both carried large lighted candles that lit the entrance of the new space.

It was a large drop into a room with a set of steep wooden stairs that led down to the stone floor below. The candles threw shadows on the floor casting some light throughout the room but there were no objects to make it looked lived in. There were no windows, no doors, no furniture, and no tapestries. With little air movement, John's nostrils immediately caught the smell of decay and rotten meat. Shackles hanging from the wall all but told John that this was to be his home for a while.

"Chain him good," said Publius to the two guards who were with him. "And don't waste any food on him."

After the guards had left and the door had closed above it was as dark as night. He heard the unmistakable noise of rats scurrying along the stone floor and immediately regretted not having his sandals with him. His toes would soon feel their teeth and that would be just the beginning he knew. The shackles hung loosely and left ample room for movement in his arms but the chains were pulled tightly enough so as to not let him sit down or reach from one hand to another. Nor could he touch his feet so as to ward off critters but he was thankful that he could scratch his nose which now tickled. Thankfully his back did not sting as it had done most of the trip and so was able to close his eyes and nod off occasionally, only to be awakened to nibbling on his feet.

"God," he said to the room as he kicked a rat away from his foot after having slept only for a few minutes. "Here I am Lord. It is I John the Baptizer. You must know who I am for it was through your words that put me here," he exclaimed rather loudly just to make sure God heard him. "Now teach me to say the right things Lord for I am nothing but a humble servant unworthy of your love and I know not what to say."

Hours slowly crept by in the darkness and he grew hungry, thirsty and cold in the damp cellar. Occasionally he would talk to God but even that became tiresome as his throat began to swell after not having anything to drink. The rat would come and go and he would kick at it as it crawled over his foot. At first, he even spoke to it but soon tired of that also. Hours of fatigue followed by only a short moments rest took its toll until finally he was too tired to even fight off the rat and he fell deeply asleep.

Herodias threw her cup across the room along with its contents of wine and smashed it and the red liquid all over the floor. "I want him drawn and quartered," she screamed once more. Every servant in the household section of the castle knew not to be seen during this time and so hid as best they could. When Herodias was furious everyone knew to stay well away.

Antipas frowned. "No one does that anymore," he said trying to placate her.

"The Romans do," she spat back. "They do everything."

"Well just because they do, doesn't mean we have to," he answered trying to sound calm and understanding. "Besides, there is no need to rip his arms and legs out. He is in the dungeon and there he will stay. We can deal with him later."

"But after what he said to me and to you and in front of our servants and your royal guard, he should be at least fed to a pack of wild dogs. No man alive should be able to do that and get away with it."

She was finally slowing down and Antipas was glad of it. It had been a rage that had lasted almost the entire morning, flinging objects, yelling, spitting and even lashing out at him with a knife. He had never seen her more angry in his life. "And he won't get away with it Herodias. I will have him beaten each day and he will be fed only on occasion and then he will be eating rat. He will have to drink out of the same bucket he defecates in and when he is at his end I will have him drowned."

She seethed as she looked at him but her heavy breathing had been replaced with a slight heaving in her chest. "That is not good enough but it will have to do, I suppose. But you make sure that he suffers daily and that he never leaves that dungeon alive."

Antipas was relieved that she had finally been placated. At last, he was able to sit down on his sofa and breathe calmly. His wine goblet had been spared and so he took a deep gulp draining the remaining liquid from it. "Why not go take a bath, my dear. It always helps to settle you down after you've been worked up."

Herodias turned, her eyes reddened with anger, and she spat at Antipas. "You will not have peace in this household until that man is dead," she barked at him just as angrily as she had before. "And don't you dare try and come to my bed until he is."

Antipas poured another full goblet and downed half of it without pause. Within minutes of Herodias heading to the baths, her servants were on the patio picking up shards of clay, cleaning up wine off the plaster and rugs, and re-righting the concrete table that she had kicked over. Luckily the mosaic tile had not been shattered or they would have had to re-lay a big part of the floor. Within a few minutes, they had all disappeared and the room had returned to normal albeit with a few less or different decorations.

Antipas had no idea what to do with the man in his cellar. He wasn't about to do any of those things that he had said he would to Herodias but he had to do something. Maybe it was too late to let him go if he agreed to say no more but he would have to decide that later. For now, he figured he would go see him in the morning and try and talk some sense into his head if he wanted to live.

It was times like these that he regretted ever marrying that spiteful woman for all she brought to this household was grief and anxiety. But he had already thrown away one wife and it would not do to discard another, although the thought of it sounded appetizing. "Maybe she will drown in the bath," he said out loud to himself and then instantly regretted it. The walls had ears and this would not do good to be reported back to her.

Looking around he decided no one had heard him and then decided after having poured another cup of wine to go visit one of his estates where he grew his grapes. That would get him out for a few days and away from her. Not wanting to have to spend another day with her he walked into the baths and caught her moving from the steam room into the hot bath itself. That is why I married her, he said to himself watching her figure as she stepped into the steaming water. Maybe I will stay, he decided suddenly ducking back behind a wall, and maybe I will do something to the prophet.

Later that evening he was on his balcony speaking to his friend Manaen and drinking a very good vintage wine. "Manaen," he asked solemnly. "Do the Romans still draw and quarter people these days?"

After a brief pause to digest the question his friend finally answered. "I'm not sure my Lord. Is there someone who needs punishing?"

Antipas shook his head up and down but didn't tell him who he was thinking of. "Herodias would like someone drawn and quartered and I have no idea how to go about it."

"I would think it would be a fairly easy thing to do although I have never seen it done. I believe you just tie each arm to a separate horse and then each leg to two other horses and then whip them all to run in different directions." He thought for a moment and then continued. "Then I suspect that as the four horses reach the ends of the ropes, the person will be drawn and quartered."

"Umm?" said Antipas pouring himself another cup of wine. "Sounds dreadful. Let's hope we never succumb to that kind of brutality."

"No, my Lord. I would hope not."

"Do you really think that the Romans still do that sort of thing?"

Manaen blinked and thought for a moment. "I saw a man crucified once," he said his nose upturned in disgust. "A big black bird was picking at his eye while he hung from his hands and feet in utter agony. It was awful."

Antipas laughed. "Well they are who they are and there's no much we can do about them, is there?"

Chapter 10 – Walking on the Sea of Galilee

Nathanael really didn't like boats. He wasn't a fisherman like Peter and Zebedee's boys. Peter loved his boat and always preferred going across the Sea of Galilee than walking around it and being the hard headed guy that he was and a favorite of Jesus, he usually got what he wanted. And thus just about every time they went out on the boat to get to somewhere Nathanael became sick.

"It's all in your head," Peter told him as the waves lifted the front of the boat just before it rolled on its side. Peter shifted his weight to allow for the roll of the boat which made it appear to Nathanael that he was floating on air. "How in the world can you get sick at sea?" he asked laughing. "You don't get sick on land do you?"

Nathanael stared at Peter with envy as his friend stood like a stone at the bow holding one hand with a rope tied to the mast and the other on his hip as he lectured him on not getting sick. He had already thrown up twice and his stomach was ready to heave again. This would be the very last time he ever road in a boat he told himself for the hundredth time. "That's easy for you to say Peter, you were born on a boat."

Peter laughed louder than ever, his eyes bright and forever darting to make sure all was alright. Everyone, including Nathanael, liked his high spirits and calm intuition. He was a born leader Nathanael thought even if he was a little impetuous. He would laugh when no one else did and rarely complained except when he thought he was right, which was often. Unlike Philip, who was always serious and trying to do as Jesus asked him, Peter was always looking for ways to do something better and usually with less work.

His powerful muscles strained at the pull of the rope when the boat rolled but Peter hung on. He was a stout man, with large arms and legs and a clean forehead where once hair grew. But he didn't care in the least. To make up for the loss of hair he had a full rich beard which stuck out in every different direction. And just as it grew freely he relished his freedom and the wild open space of the sea that was his home. "If you can control your mind, Nathanael," Peter explained, "you can control everything. Look at all the fish in the sea and none of them are seasick," he laughed again even louder.

But it didn't help. His stomach ached, he tasted bile in his throat, and his head swam around as if he had had too much wine. It didn't matter what Peter said, he was miserable and there was nothing that he could say that would calm his body at this moment. "Right now I would rather be dead," he said grieving horribly as he held tightly to the boat's side with arms and hands.

Peter laughed again. He was having fun at Nathanael's expense because he couldn't understand how anyone could be sick on the water. He had been born on this sea and as a child, his father had taken him out to the deep many a time. He remembered as a child having ridden plenty a hard squall with waves blowing over the bow without ever having remembered worrying about their making it through. He was fishing by five years old and hauling in nets at the age of eight. No one was more comfortable at sea than he and he relished it.

"Hang in there Nathanael," Philip yelled as the ship heaved into the air and then slammed against the next wave. The look on Nathanael's face said it all and Philip felt for him. He moved closer and thrust his arm around his shoulder. "It will be over soon. These things never last very long."

Nathanael shook his head up and down as if he agreed but it was just a pretense for he doubted seriously if it would ever be over. Ever since he had given his life up with John to follow Jesus it had been one sensational moment after another and he was growing weary of what was happening. Jesus was going around healing everyone in sight. Whether blind or lame or crippled, he healed them all and asked for nothing in return. Nathanael was dumbfounded at what all was taking place and he had no way to put it in perspective.

The other eleven disciples didn't seem to be relishing the excitement as Peter had been for they were mostly hunkered down in the belly of the boat or hanging over the side as Nathanael was doing. "Well I hope not much longer," he moaned. "I don't think I can make it much longer."

Suddenly Philip stood up as Peter yelled as loud as he could, "look, a ghost."

James who had been sitting next to the mast stood up next followed by Judas and then John. Then within a few seconds, everyone was up and looking out over the whitecaps trying to see what Peter had seen. Nathanael was one of the last but as he finally was on his feet when he saw what seemed to be a person on the water walking towards them.

"What is it," yelled James incredulously, the waves splashing out over them soaking all their clothes.

"I don't know," Peter yelled back sounding less confident than he had just a few minutes before. "Is it a ghost?"

Then Philip who had been peering hard into the darkness began to yell. "Look, it's Jesus. It's not a ghost. It's Jesus on the water."

Nathanael wiped his eyes and peered again into the darkness. There was indeed someone walking on the waves but surely it wasn't Jesus. No one could walk on water. 'Are you sure," he yelled over the sounds of the sea.

Peter yelled again, water and wind splashing across his face. "Yes, it is Jesus," he yelled pointing at the figure a few yards from then. "I am sure of it. Look."

Many nodded, some yelled in agreement, but Nathanael just wasn't sure who or what it was. "But no one can walk on water," he said yelling at Philip over the crashing of the waves.

Philip grabbed his shoulder and pulled him towards the railing. "Look, it is him. Can't you see his face?"

Nathanael saw his face and agreed that it looked like Jesus but this was a man walking on water and no one could do that. He wanted to believe but wasn't ready to. "I'm not sure," he said in reply.

Then suddenly Peter yelled in his deep masculine voice. "Jesus, if it is you, command me to come to you on the water."

Everyone's eyes darted to Peter. It was just like Peter to say something like this; impetuous and even foolhardy. He was standing one foot on the rail with his hand outstretched to Jesus who was now only about ten paces away. The boat continued to roll but suddenly seemed lesser than before. The waves seemed to not cause Jesus to rock nor were they washing over him as they had the boat just a moment before. In fact, to Nathanael, it appeared that everything around Jesus was calm and the closer they got the calmer they got too.

Then to Nathanael's utter amazement he heard Jesus yell back to him. "Come, Peter, come to me."

They all fell quiet and in awe watched as Peter looked around as if needing support and then when getting none he stepped out anyway over the side of the boat and onto the water. Then as if all time had stopped and nothing in the world meant anything any longer Peter took a step and was walking on water. Nathanael looked up and saw Jesus, his arms stretched out to Peter calling him across the waves and then his eyes darted back to Peter to see what he was doing. Amazingly Peter stood on the water with one hand still on the boat, wide-eyed and terrified.

"Come, Peter," said Jesus softly, his voice being heard easily by everyone despite the rain and the waves hitting the boat. "Walk to me."

Again Nathanael's eyes locked onto Peter watching intently as his hand slowly lifted off the rail, his eyes darting from the boat to Jesus and back again. And then he took one step towards Jesus, stepping lightly as if the surface was made of glass. And then he took another and that's when he froze. Nathanael could see the fear rising in Peter's eyes, the first time he had ever seen him scared, and he wanted to reach out to Peter but he did not know how without drowning himself. As if the water below suddenly came alive, the sea slowly began to rise up over Peter's sandals. Sensing doom, Peter stretched out his arms as far as they could to reach Jesus but he was too far away and when he realized this, his eyes looked down into the depths below, and suddenly he began to sink.

"Lord, save me," he yelled to Jesus in terror as he started to go down, but before the water was at his chest Jesus was there to lift him up. Nathanael's heart seemed to have stopped that instant. He made himself inhale so that he would breathe again as he watched the scene out in the water. Jesus was holding him out of the water and yet Jesus was on the water as well. Nathanael glanced back at Philip hoping for some explanation but got none.

Then Nathanael heard Jesus whisper to Peter, "Oh you of little faith," as he held him in his arms tightly so as to keep him from sinking into the abyss. Nathanael was dumbfounded. He searched the faces of everyone in the boat for disbelief but found none. Was he the only one that couldn't believe what had happened he wondered? How in the name of God could he walk on water? And then he noticed it had quit raining.

"Philip," he whispered. "It has quit raining. And the sea has subsided. Everything is quite. So quiet, that I even heard Jesus speaking to Peter way out there."

"So did I," Philip whispered back. "There is not a wave on the water and the wind has stopped. Do you think Jesus had anything to do with it?"

"I don't know anything anymore," Nathanael murmured in disbelief. "I am waiting to wake up from this at any moment."

"Well if it is a dream, it has been very real. I doubt anyone will believe this when we tell them."

Nathanael shook his head. "You can tell them but I'm not saying a word."

The next day they landed in the territory of Gerasenes and Nathanael was more than happy to finally be on land. "My God, that was awful," he told Philip as he kneeled in the mud. "I have never been so sick in my life."

"Yes, but wasn't it exciting to see Jesus walking on the water?"

Nathanael wanted to ask if he really thought he had walked on water but decided that he would just not say anything about it to anyone. Yes, he had seen Jesus heal all kinds of diseases and infirmities but this was different. This time, Jesus took on nature and defeated it. If he could do that to the wind and the water what else could he do he wondered? What kind of man was he following? Who was he and where did he get these mystical powers that he uses here and there as easily as the wind blows the leaves across the field?

"Well come on Nathanael, let's move it or we will be left behind."

They walked for better part of the morning when they came upon a village nestled against the lake, which on this side was named Gennesaret, which also happened to be the name of the village. Nathanael had been there once as a child when his father was looking for work. Nothing had changed it appeared to him as little did anywhere around these parts he imagined. But instead of going into the village, Jesus decided to rest near the lake at a point that jutted out near them.

The brothers shared some bread they had bought in a town they had passed through earlier and so they all quietly sat on the shore eating and watching the fishing boats quietly throwing their nets and bringing up little. "This will be a bad place to try and feed a crowd," said James looking out at the boats. "I haven't seen anyone pull up any fish yet."

"They are fishing in the wrong place," said Peter pointing out to the other shore. "The lake looks too shallow where they are. I would move to deeper waters."

"How come it is that fishermen know more than any other fisherman?" asked Nathanael to no one in particular but receiving a few jeers.

"You are fishers of fish now," suddenly Jesus said looking around to each of their faces. It was that look that he gave them when he was about to speak about something that concerned them. He often did that but Nathanael wasn't sure what he was trying to get across. Then he nodded slowly and smiled slightly, something he also did quite often. "But soon I will make you fishers of men."

Nathanael knew it was coming. The last line was always about them and what they could expect but it was never ever clear. He wanted to ask what that meant to be fishers of men but no one else seemed to be confused, and so he said nothing. It was another one of those Jesus comments that seemed to mean only something that he knew about and they didn't. It was like a puzzle every time he opened his mouth, Nathanael murmured to himself. Even Peter looked as if he understood but he doubted it. In fact, he doubted that anyone knew the meaning to his words. But Jesus never seemed to worry about whether they did or not, because he continued to say things and they kept listening.

It was a little before noon and Nathanael had been dozing on and off when they first heard the high shrieks not too far from where they were sitting. To his surprise, Jesus rose and began to walk towards the noise which triggered the rest of the small band to do likewise. He saw a large hairy man who appeared to have very few clothes on, if anything at all, in the midst of a graveyard yelling at something or someone, his arms lashing against the air as if he were trying to fight off someone. Nathanael smiled to himself and darted his eyes away from the nakedness as they got closer.

Jesus approached the man who Nathanael guessed by now was an idiot or crazy in some fashion. No one in their right mind would be screaming among the tombs throwing his arms in the air without any clothes on. He wondered why Jesus even bothered with this man. Then suddenly without warning the crazy man turned and saw Jesus standing behind him and Nathanael feared that he might hit him. But instead, the man suddenly fell to his knees.

"What have you to do with me, Jesus, son of the Most High," he yelled at the top of his lungs causing Nathanael to jump. "I beg you, do not torment me," he finished, his head bowed low as everyone else held their breaths in anticipation.

Nathanael's eyes were locked on Jesus for he knew now that something was going to happen. Jesus was like that, always sensing everything around him and somehow knowing what to do about it. And as always he was in complete control of himself, his voice calm and lowered as he spoke. Nathanael had seen him sooth those who were frightened or scared of him over and over. He had a way about him that won over people no matter what the circumstance. Even the Jewish hierarchy as much as they tried, could never shake him.

"What is your name," Jesus asked compassionately as if somehow understanding the man's anguish. Somehow Nathanael decided that he knew what was causing the man to behave this way and he was somehow going to fix it.

"The man suddenly yelled out 'Legion', making Nathanael step back a half step. He glanced up for an instant to see Andrew grasping onto Peter's shoulder but they stood fast. And then the man yelled again but this time, Nathanael held his own. "Please do not send us to the abyss," the man pleaded.

His answer struck Nathanael as being strange. Why in the world did he say that his name was legion, and where was the abyss, and why would Jesus throw him in it? Nathanael's eyes were now

154

locked on the creature who was now looking at Jesus intently, white foam building at the corners of his mouth, his eyes red with anger and lack of sleep, and as his hands and shoulders shaking terrifically in spasms as he pushed his large fist against the grass he was kneeling on. It was a pathetic sight, this large freaky man kneeling on all fours pleading with Jesus to set him free but what that meant he had no idea.

The the man looked up, the foam dripping from his mouth, his head shaking back and forth like a mad man. "Then send us into the swine," he begged him as he pointed at the small herd near the lake. Nathanael glanced over to see the pigs huddled together feeding on something but he didn't keep his eyes there long. Something was about to happen and he wanted to see it for himself.

Then Jesus began to speak and Nathanael's eyes moved back to him to see what he would say. "I will it," was all he said and at that moment, the man dropped face first into the grass completely still. Nathanael glanced at the man and then heard an awful noise where he had just been looking moments before. Without warning of any kind, the swine were suddenly all running head first into the lake, falling over each other as they went diving into the peaceful water.

"What in the world," asked Nathanael to no one, staring out into the lake where dozens of pigs now lay floating dead in the water. It was the strangest sight he had ever seen.

Then the man stirred, his hands pushing against the ground lifting his head up. He looked at Jesus first and then turning his head he saw the rest of us. He sat up shaking his head slowly as to clear his mind. Peter, always looking for something to do came up to them and placed his cloak on the man's back so as to cover his nakedness. "Thank you, sir," he said to Jesus.

Jesus smiled and nodded his appreciation. Then standing he looked at the hillside where a dozen or more of the town's people had gathered to look at the dead swine still floating against the shore. People were talking among themselves, some pointing to the swine, some pointing to Jesus, but all discussing the strange event of the crazy man and the swine. The man was up now on his feet but had not taken his eyes off of Jesus.

"I have been this way sir for years with no one to help me. This demoniac that you have driven into the swine I have lived with in nakedness day and night and in the rain and in the cold. They have tried, but no one has ever been able to help me." He paused for a moment wiping his mouth of the foam that had been there. "Please tell me sir who you are so that I may follow you and praise your name."

Jesus smiled back and placed his hand on the man shoulder. Nathanael could see real joy in his eyes for what he had done for this man. "Return home, my son, and recount what God has done for you."

The man shook his head in agreement but seemed disappointed none the less. He placed his hand on Jesus' hand and then turned and walked away. They watched in quiet, each trying to understand, but none being able to do so.

Chapter 11 – Antipas' Dungeon

It was two days before John again saw the light again. He had no idea if it was night or day but suddenly a glimmer of light from a candle illumined the room causing him to raise his tired head and eyes to the staircase. He blinked several times to make sure he wasn't dreaming for he had had this dream before only to be disappointed when he awoke. But this time, it was real.

It must be Antipas John presumed as the man with the candle slowly negotiated the shadowy staircase. Then he watched as his nemeses walked up to him, their eyes locked on each other as they had before. Antipas looked tired, his eyes reddish and without the supreme confidence that he had shown the other day. Suddenly he pulled his leg back and flung it towards John but instead of hitting John he caught the rat with a hard blow to its head and flung it to the other wall. He did this all with his eyes still fixed on John.

"Are you hungry," he asked softly holding up something in front of John. "I have some bread and some cheese and a hardboiled egg in the basket."

John tried to speak but his throat was too dry to say much. After several tries of mouthing words he swallowed and tried again. "Water," he said hoarsely. "I need water."

Antipas had no water but took the four or five steps over to the stairs and yelled up to the guards. "Bring me a bucket of water," he said and then returned.

They waited without saying anything until eventually, the guard came stumbling down the stairs as quickly as he could with a large bucket of water sloshing about and over the rim onto the floor. Antipas looked angrily at the guard and then dismissed him before turning back to John. "Here," he said handing him the water-filled bucket. "Drink."

John drank nearly half the bucket before finally stopping. He threw his head back against the hard wall and whispered, "Thank You," and then closed his eyes for a moment.

Antipas felt bad for the man. "I am sorry they haven't taken better care of you," he said. "I will make sure they do so in the future."

John weakly smiled and asked for the piece of bread which he then tenderly tried to eat. Antipas watched him without saying anything handing him the water bucket when he needed it and then peeling the egg for him and watching him dispose of it. Finally, John ate the cheese and finished the rest of the water.

"Thank you," said John whipping his mouth. "That was very good."

"You will get more. And I will get you a cot to lie on so that you can get some decent sleep."

John again shook his head up and down as in thanks. "You are a good man, you know," he said to Antipas slightly smiling. "But your sins cast a giant shadow over you, your wife and your kingdom and they will destroy them all unless you repent."

"But why are you after me?" he asked dumbfounded. "What have I done to receive this outburst from you?"

"It's not me," John answered. "God sent me to tell you that you must repent of your sins. You are only punishing the messenger. I have nothing to do with it."

Antipas shook his head angrily. "Poppycock," he said throwing his hands against the side of his head in a fury. "You are not from here," he shouted although he was only a foot away from him. "And my people tell me that you have been thrown out of more than a few synagogues and towns in the south and that you were also among the Essenes for a while near the Dead Sea. So you see I do know who you are and I would doubt that your pedigree places you in the company of God."

This time, John was the calm one. "Yes, I can see where you may not see me as a messenger from God. But whether I am or not, you have a storm cloud hanging over your family and your kingdom and if you do not do something about it, it will destroy you."

"How do you know that," Antipas shouted again his arms now thrashing about in frustration. "How do you know anything, you water creature? Tell me so that I can tell my wife."

"I told you, God told me," he answered calmly and quietly.

Antipas held his clenched fist near to John's face as to hit him, then abruptly dropped his arm to his side and closed his mouth and just stared at the man on the wall. And when he spoke, he did so more calmly. "And why is God so interested in my affairs?" he asked.

"Because we are living in the days of the awakening when you will see and come to judge the righteous one whom your people will hang from a tree, and that is why God has sent me here, to warn you that what you will do will have vast consequences for you and your kingdom."

Antipas was dumbstruck. He had no idea what John was talking about but it scared him none the less. He wanted to say something but no words would come and so after a moment, he turned and walked over to the stairs. "Guard," he yelled then waited while the soldier came stumbling down the stairs. "Take him out of those chains, find him a bed, give him a blanket and plenty to eat day and night with fresh water and empty his waste."

The guard gasped at the last command. "Clean his bucket my Lord," he asked stupidly.

Antipas shook his head. "If I come down here and see any waste sitting in a bucket or if I find out he has not been well fed or hasn't had water I will take your skin off your back. Do you understand?" he asked his voice steady but forceful. "And make sure there are no rats running around."

The guard shook his head as if he had and then immediately ran up the stairs. Antipas came back over to John. "God, uh? Well, maybe it was God who sent you and maybe it wasn't. We shall see."

For two days John slept quietly on his bed resting the sores on his feet from the rat bites and the puffy blisters on his back from the lashing. Now free from the chains he was able to wash his wounds and along with the fresh food and water he began to feel better. As promised the guards kept his waste emptied and his bucket full of fresh water and even got rid of the rats that were always trying to get to his food. He still could not count the days or nights but with good hard sleep, it made no difference. Soon he began to feel healthy.

During the next few weeks, John heard Antipas' voice talking to the guards inquiring about how he was doing. On several occasions, he actually came down part way on the stairs to look in on him but said nothing and soon disappeared. During that time, John's food became better and he grew stronger both physically and mentally. Then one day he heard footsteps and was surprised when Antipas did not stop on the steps but instead came all the way to the floor.

"How are you feeling," asked Antipas. He was holding two candleholders. One was a lit candle in it which Antipas had used to negotiate the stairs and the other was a fresh never been lit candle.

"Much better, thanks to you," he said nodding his head. He was sitting on his cot with the blanket over his shoulders for warmth. "You have been very kind to me."

"Here's you a candle. I will have the guards light it each morning so that you will know it is day and put it out each evening after dark. That way you will know when it is day or night. I'm sorry that is all I can do for you. Herodias thinks you are still chained to the wall and being eaten to death by rats."

"I was just about I'm afraid," he said smiling widely for the first time since Antipas had met him.

"Well, yes," he muttered somewhat embarrassed. "It seems that was my fault. Again, my apology."

John leaned back against the wall. "Have you thought any more about what I said?" he asked.

Antipas looked tired again to John but not as red-eyed as he had the last time they had talked together. "In fact, I have," he said. "It seems I can think of nothing else."

"And?"

"The question still remains," Antipas replied then stopped to formulate his words. "How can I be sure that this message is from God and not from some lowly unpolished evangelist who has been thrown out of every town he has preached in?"

"Because, I was told by God to tell you this."

"But how do I know you are for real," he asked throwing his hands up in disgust. "Put yourself in my position. Would you believe you?"

John laughed. "I see what you mean," he said. "And I hold no grudge against you for seeing me in this light. However, let's look at this from a different direction. Let's say that I am the High Priest Caiaphas and it was him who told you that you have committed a sin before God for marrying your half-sister. What would you do then?"

Antipas thought for a moment. "I would have him thrown in a well," he said lightly laughing. And then he looked serious. "No one tells me that," he demanded. "No one."

"But I did," added John.

"And look where you are," he corrected him. "But back to your point. If this is true, what you say. Then how come the High Priest Caiaphas hasn't been here knocking on my door ordering me to repent?"

John thought for a moment. He looked at Antipas, his fingers stroking his beard in thoughtfulness as he waited for his answer. It was a good rebuttal and one he hadn't thought of. No one was holier than Caiaphas, so how come he hadn't given Antipas the same message? It was an answer he would have to think about.

"Well you think about it, my friend and we will discuss at a different time. My wife is throwing me a birthday party next week and I am up to my neck with requests from her to buy this or this and none of which is truly needed."

"I hope to be invited," John added laughing at his joke.

Antipas laughed also. "Yes, that would be a scream, wouldn't it? Herodias would choke on her quail."

Unexpectedly, Antipas came back the next evening and sat down next to John with a thoughtful expression on his face. As he had lately, his eyes looked red and swollen and his face mellow. Even his typically tidy beard was shaggy as he stroked it with his hands.

"You look tired my Lord," John said as he sat beside him.

Antipas laughed seemed to be distant to John. "It's my wife. She is uncontrollable at this moment with the birthday thing coming up. I do wish it would get over."

"This too will pass," John said sympathetically.

Antipas smiled weakly and nodded. "I like you, John. You're a good man despite your barrage upon me and my family."

"But my Lord," he explained. "I am just trying to set you right with God. I would be amiss if I didn't take my calling seriously."

"Yes, yes," Antipas countered as if he were exasperated with the topic. "I know." There was a slight pause before he began again. John was certain that Antipas had come for something more than just to pass the time. "What do you know about a preacher named Jesus?" he finally asked casually as if it meant nothing to him.

John suddenly grew enthusiastic. Until now they had been focusing on Antipas' troubles, especially his marriage but now he had brought up something that was near to John's heart. "Jesus of Nazareth?" he asked for clarification.

Antipas frowned. "Why I am not sure. He's a preacher of sorts and many say a healer, or that's what some claim he is. And yes I do think he's been roaming throughout the Galilee region so he could be from Nazareth."

"Yes, that would be him," John answered. "What have you heard?"

Antipas ran his fingers across his beard as he did often when he was thinking. "Well, I'm concerned that he is attracting a following. Every time he enters a town or village throngs come out to hear him."

"Is he speaking harshly against the empire or the emperor?" John asked suspiciously.

"No. Nor of me as you did." The slight to John was not given with any malice and John ignored it. "But he preaches, from what I understand, of peace and God and brotherly love." He paused for a moment as if he was contemplating the words. Then he looked up. "Have you ever met him," he asked.

"Once," John answered remembering when he had baptized Jesus. "I believe, as you have heard, that he is indeed a man of God. He is the one that I have been speaking of for so long who will save the people of Israel."

Antipas twisted his mind racing with questions. "Save us from what?" he asked.

"From you, and Caiaphas, and Rome," he answered succinctly. "I believe that he is the Messiah, the one chosen by God to free his people."

"Well we shall see," he said in return. "I doubt very seriously that the chosen one of God will have come from Nazareth and would be an itinerate preacher with no means."

"Like Moses," asked John slightly smiling in the comparison? "Wasn't he of no account when God called him to free our people from Egypt?"

Antipas stood up. He was about to say something but decided against it and left. John was sure that he had gone too far but he had never stopped short of telling the truth. If Antipas held that against him then so be it. The last thing he heard for a week was the door slamming shut behind him.

Antipas leaned against the wall next to the door he had just shut. "You know what," he said to John who could not hear him. "You are my only friend in the world," he said, his eyes filling with tears. And then he laughed. "The only man unafraid of me in the world and who dares tell me what I know to be true." He said again to himself as he wiped his eyes with his sleeve. "I should draw and quarter you as Herodias wants. But I can't." He paused looking around the great room where he had ruled for so long and yet had been so unhappy. "Because then I would be killing my only friend."

Chapter 12 – Salome

Herodias pulled the brush once more through the golden hair of her daughter Salome. Half a dozen candles flickered from the light breeze that filtered through the window facing the northern plains. Salome tugged against the tangles but Herodias didn't care. She was determined to have the most beautiful daughter in all of Perea present on the morrow at her husband's birthday and didn't care what it took to make it happen.

"That hurts mother," she complained as she pulled her head against the brush.

"Well since you won't do it I have to, so get over it."

She was a beautiful girl. Herodias envied her tight chin and full lips. She had long since lost the tightness that was her youth and often wished she had it back. She still stole glances from men other than her husband but they all knew to leave her alone. She was the king's wife and that was off limits. But she was still thrilled when a handsome man paid attention to her now and then. But Salome was shapely for her age and had beautiful skin and hair. No one would compete with her and that was a good thing for she would soon be marrying, although that idiot of a future husband couldn't come to the party.

While at her task trying to straighten her daughter's hair, Herodias thought about the following day's events. She wished sometimes that she hadn't married Antipas for she had always thought of him as a stick in the mud old tyrant. He had seduced her when she was younger and she had fallen for it because of his charm and wealth but the charm didn't last. This no longer bothered her as it did at first because he kept busy and out of her way, but it did bother her when he did not treat her like his queen in front of other important people. Often than not, he would cast her aside as if she was not even there, leaving her to fend for herself as if she were a consort.

But tomorrow she swore she was not going to let herself be tossed aside. She would make sure that the highest ranking guest sat near her, including that awful Pontius Pilate who had unfortunately accepted their invitation. She would just have to make sure that she placed that awful wife of his away from her. Her husband would be a good choice to sit next to her and then they could keep each other company. She remembered how much he detested her on their first visit and it pleased her to know that she could make them squirm at the table together.

Herodias had been working the invitations for weeks and except for a few minor officials, everyone had accepted. Her staff was in a panic over her instructions that seemed to change from day to day, and the food list and preparation were immensely complicated. Her staff had already bought hundreds of blocks of goat cheese, half a dozen young lambs, a hundred live quail and as many plump turtle doves, a dozen stout deer for succulent venison, as much veal as she could get, plenty of fine fruits and vegetables to feed everyone in the city, and one hundred stone large amphorae's of wine holding no less than fifty quarts each. Her biggest problem was where to store and prepare all of this which caused her to hire dozens of servants from all over the city to help her cook and serve this vast array of foods.

There was no one better than Herodias at throwing this large of a party but none the less, her temper and stress grew exponentially the larger the party was to be. Everyone knew, especially Antipas, not to speak with her while she was focusing on her lists.

"You know that you can hear her all the way in the alley from here," Antipas told Salome as he sat on the patio with her eating some honey and flat bread for breakfast the next day. "Thank goodness today is the day, huh? It will soon be over and we will have peace once again"

Salome could have cared less what her mother served or the problems she was having doing so. The only thing she cared about was who was coming, and to her chagrin, she had learned just that morning that no one her age had been invited. She would have to spend the entire evening smiling at a bunch of old people and pretending to be having a wonderful time. She dreaded having to dress in the horrible black gown that her mother had made for her, for it fit much too tightly and would be uncomfortable the entire day. She would have missed the entire thing if she could get away with it.

Antipas, on the other hand, was just plain bored but there was nothing he could do but just get through it. As parties went it appeared it would be a success with everyone coming that Herodias had invited. He would have to spend some time with the Prefect Pontius Pilate but that was not all bad. He hadn't been to Machaerus before and it wouldn't hurt to show off another city that Antipas had rebuilt. Like Tiberius, he had redesigned it to look a lot like any modern Roman city with all its amenities and sporting venues. The baths weren't quite as luxuries as they were in Tiberius but that was because of the hot springs found there. Here they had to heat the water with hot rocks and that took time and a lot of expense.

They both sat in robes quietly picking at the food that had been served earlier. Herodias suddenly appeared through the doorway and plopped down on a couch near her husband and daughter. She looked frazzled thought Antipas but he knew that she would look spectacular before guests began arriving shortly. The entire event wouldn't start before the sun set but it wouldn't finish until the next morning after the sun rose. There would be three full meals served over that time and a lot of wine drunk.

"I will discharge every one of the servants and start over after tomorrow," she spat. "I can get none of them to do anything that I say and everything they do is wrong."

"It will be alright sweetheart," he said in as soothing voice as he could muster. It was the same thing she said after every party so it did not bother him to hear her complain about them. "So far I think things are going well. The courtyard has never looked finer."

"And what would you know about it?" she shot back at him. "I have done nothing but slave over this birthday of yours for a month mind you and am just about fed up with it. So don't try and patronize me."

Antipas sighed and placed another piece of bread in his mouth covered with honey. He loved this stuff so much that he had hired some beekeepers to make sure that they had ample honey whenever they could get it. He glanced at Salome and noted that she wasn't in the least bit interested in her mother's outbreak either and thus had nothing to say. She sipped a small cup of watered downed wine and then sat up.

"I think I will go out for a while," she said yawning. "I am bored here."

"And that's because you do nothing all day," replied Herodias her mood growing ever fouler.

Antipas frowned. "Maybe I will go along with you," he asked of Salome. "We can walk the shops this morning while your mother finishes her last minute items."

Herodias stood up just as abruptly as she had sat down. "Well you two do whatever you want but you had better be back in time to bathe and dress before our guests arrive."

He didn't go with Salome as she wouldn't have enjoyed his company and he didn't really want to go see the shops. Instead, he went into the dungeon to make a short visit with John. He hadn't seen him in several days and wanted to see how he was doing. Often it was damp and cold down there and he had no desire for John to get sick and die from exposure.

"How are you, my friend," he asked stepping off the stair bottom landing. As always John was sitting up waiting for him to come down once he heard the door from above open. He could tell the difference by now between the guards who were noisy and sloppy and Antipas who almost seemed to be so quiet so as to not disturb John.

"Do you think we could go out for a while some evening?" he asked full of hope that he could at least see the stars for one evening.

Antipas wondered why he hadn't thought of that himself. "Of course," he replied smiling. "After this awful party of mine that is really not mine, we will take a long walk through the ramparts. I will, of course, have to sneak you out so that Herodias doesn't see us. I think she would have a cow if she saw me walking you around the palace."

"Yes, of course."

Suddenly Antipas smiled. "I do wish I could invite you to my birthday party. Everyone inside and outside the country who is anyone will be there. But of course, that is not practical even if you did promise to not say anything about Herodias."

"I quite understand," he said in agreement.

"Anyway, things tend to get a little lively with all the wine being drunk and it never fails that people always stay until dawn. I hope we don't disturb you too much. I'll try and come down sometime and bring you some of Herodias' veal and gravy. It is out of this world."

John lightly laughed. "Just don't let her know who it's for."

Antipas smiled back at him. "You know John; I have come to like you a lot. You are a good and holy man and even though you tell me things I don't want to hear, you have always spoken your convictions." He paused while he thought some more. John said nothing. "That is a hard thing to find in my position. Unfortunately, you have struck a nerve with my wife and so I am in a quandary as to what to do with you."

"You could let me go," suggested John, no longer smiling. "You can't keep me here forever."

"No, you are right. I can't. But," he started as he stood up. "We shall talk about this later. For now, I have to finish dressing and get prepared to meet the guest. My wife tells me there are hundreds coming. I hope not, but who knows." He stopped at the staircase and turned back towards John. "Take care my friend, and have a restful night."

"Thank you my Lord."

And they did arrive by the dozens in coaches and on horseback and even a few by foot. The women wore beautiful long garments of many colors and fine materials, none of which were alike, and they were all adorned with expensive necklaces, piercings, and arm bracelets made of turquoise and silver and gold. Many of the women also wore wigs of all shapes and colors and often as not wore rouge on their cheeks and lips, although the older women thought this a scandal. Some of the men wore Roman togas with purple accents but mostly they wore handsome cotton garments with shirts that were also multicolored and hung below their waist. Some of the men also wore jewelry and even a few of the younger brave ones wore wigs. Antipas wore only his simplest white robe and little jewelry. It appeared to him that everyone was trying to be someone other than they were.

"If I ever have to wear a wig, stab me," said Antipas to a Sanhedrin judge standing next to him as they watched the guest arrived. The judge was dressed similarly to Antipas.

"I hope that will not be anytime soon," he replied.

It was about the closest thing that would resemble a joke thought Antipas glancing at the aged wrinkled man next to him. He had been a judge for as long as Antipas had been king or Tetrarch as the Romans preferred. Most of the visitors, in fact, had addressed him as 'Your Highness' as they had greeted him and similarly to his wife who sparkled when they did. Of course, Pilate did not. In fact, he rarely used his title at all but just addressed him as Antipas or his friend.

The first meal was full of rich foods, plenty of wine, dancing women, music, and acrobats. Herodias had spared no expense which Antipas knew would be devastating to his coffers when he got the bill. Everything was arranged so that people could sit or stand and still see all the entertainment she had to offer. And the wine poured freely with servants moving about making sure that every cup was full and that no one went thirsty. Antipas decided that he would take some veal down to John later when he felt he would have an easier time sneaking away.

Herodias as always was in charge and as she had done previously to every event thus far she clapped her hands for everyone's attention and then without saying a word pointed at the musicians who began to play a very sensuous melody. Antipas looked around expectedly waiting for some more dancers to show off their bottoms and flip their hair around but this time, only one person walked in. It was Salome in her black layered garment that accented her youthful body and golden hair.

Antipas was stunned for he had no idea that this was going to happen. Eagerly anticipating what she was going to do, he sat down on the end of a couch and sipped his wine as his eyes locked on the beautiful figure before him. Gold and silver flew all around as her arms swung through the air almost invisible because of the black garment she wore. Her head flung her braided hair from side to side as her hips matched pace; the whole package seemingly driving out in every direction including her feet that twirled magically as if almost on air.

It was not like Antipas to be so involved in a dancing girl but Salome was magically pulling him into her world. She had been taught how to move her body and do other womanly things by her mother who did not want a husband to give her back because she didn't know how to please him. She twirled endlessly around, her garments flaring about her well above any modesty height and the crowd loved it, and so did he. Glancing around the room he could tell that everyone was captivated with his daughter. It had been a long time that he could remember when he was enthralled by watching a woman dance, especially as one as sensuous as he had been watching.

The performance seemed endless but to his dismay eventually she stopped, almost crashing to the floor showing off more than some of her legs. Everyone was silent as eyes looked towards him as to what he thought; after all, it was his daughter who had caught the attention of everyone in the room. Suddenly he stood up and began to clap and once he started everyone else joined in enthusiastically. Herodias, unlike anything she had ever done before, ran out into the center of the room and threw her arms around Salome.

The clapping stopped and everyone again looked towards Antipas who was staring at her thighs that were now uncomfortably bare. "What a lovely surprise for my birthday," he shouted to everyone as he pulled his eyes away and walked across the floor offering his hand to the girl. She took it and rose from the floor leaving her mother to herself. He walked around the room leading her around like a show horse so that everyone could see how proud he was of her.

Suddenly he felt moved at all the attention he was getting. He had not felt adored by his people for many years with all the strife between the Romans and the Jews. He was often seen as being on the Romans side and even if it weren't true his dealings with them caused much of the masses to turn from him. But now was a moment to bask in his glory. He looked around and his eyes caught the stare of Pontius Pilate and Antipas smiled knowing exactly what he was going to do.

In his most powerful strongest kingly voice he announced to everyone and to the girl, "I am so delighted that I am at a loss for words," he said. Then he smiled widely at the crowd as if he had an idea. Then he turned towards her. "What is it that you would ask of me?" he said softly gazing into her eyes and holding on to both her hands. Then unexpectedly his head turned towards the crowd, her hand still in his as he spoke loudly. "Ask of me whatever you wish and I will grant it to you."

The crowd applauded wildly in anticipation of what she would ask for. She looked up into his face and blushed. "Anything girl," he reiterated. "I will grant you whatever you ask of me, even to half my kingdom."

She obviously had no idea what to ask for, nor would anyone have had at that moment. Then she then turned her face to Herodias who had remained on the floor, all attention having been taken from her. But as soon as she saw her daughter eyeing her in confusion she motioned to her with her finger to come to her side.

Antipas watched the two women whispering which made the anticipation of the crowd even greater than what it had been. The girl's head snapped back from her mother's ear and she looked at her horribly for a moment before Herodias pulled her back next to her cheek. They spoke some more until finally the girl shook her head in agreement and rose from the floor. Herodias did likewise but then moved away from the center to give separation between her and her daughter. Antipas watched all of this suspiciously after seeing the look on Salome's face when she had first spoken to her mother.

Salome came back to Antipas and looked up into his waiting stare. Everyone was holding their breath in anticipation, as was Antipas. "I would like for you to give me at once the head of John the Baptist on a platter," she said.

Antipas' shocked face darted from hers to her mother who was smiling gleefully on the other side of the room. It was her doing, he told himself. She was the one who put Salome up to this. He was about to refuse when he noticed everyone looking at him. Many knew through Herodias that Antipas had had John locked up for months in his dungeon but no one knew if he was still alive or dead. Now they knew that he was alive and that Antipas had promised in front of everyone to take his head. Pilate smiled broadly at his host's predicament as if he were enjoying the moment.

Antipas was torn as he had never been torn before. In fact, he would just as easily have traded John's head for Herodias' for putting this idea in their daughter's ear. But he had been trapped by her and now everyone was staring and waiting for his approval, and there was nothing he could do about it. Woe is the king who went back on his word he remembered his father having told him once.

He straightened his back and looked around until he found who he was looking for nestled deep behind the crowd. "Manaen," he commanded to his long friend and confidant who he had invited to the party despite his wife's objection. "Come here."

Manaen moved through the crowd and stepped next to Antipas whose face was sullen. He could see his king's hesitation but waited for him to speak. "Do as the girl ask," he said as calmly as he could.

The crowd murmured softly as Manaen looked hesitantly at his king and then withdrew. Some time went by and few said a word. Most eyes were on Herodias and her daughter Salome as they waited to see what was to happen. Herodias was beginning to think that she had spoiled the whole thing by her request and she was doing everything she could to get people to talk to each other but to the very person they all waited quietly in anticipation of seeing the head of John the Baptist on a platter. Then suddenly, to everyone's surprise, there was a scream as one of the women guests nearest to the entrance saw the eyes of John staring up from a platter with his lifeless head sitting in his own blood.

At first, there was a faint buzz as the guest murmured their surprise and anguish between each other at seeing the bearded face staring up. The guards waited until Antipas nodded before walking the platter across the room to him. Those who were in the way or near Antipas stepped back, many placing hands across their mouths in disgust. Even Antipas grimaced at the sight as the guards finally neared him but he held his emotions. Looking down at his old friend he hated that he had been tricked into ordering such a thing to happen. But there he was and nothing could change it now. He looked peaceful Antipas thought as tears blurred his eyes, and he immediately regretted not being able to say goodbye to his old friend or not having brought him some of the veal he had promised.

He wondered what John had thought when two men with a long sword came down the stairs instead of him.

"Take it to the girl," he said sadly then turned away.

Salome gasped at the sight and quickly threw her hands over her eyes and buried her face in her mother's breast. "Give it to her mother," yelled Antipas to the guards from across the room. "She's the one who wanted it."

Only Herodias smiled as the platter was presented to her.

Chapter 13– Son of David

As they traveled throughout the region, Jesus healed many and spoke of peace to the people from morning until sundown. At each village and town, the people would bring those sick and the infirmed, the crippled and the blind, to them and Jesus would heal them all. And of course, as he healed he spoke to the crowds in his soothing voice, the one that Nathanael had come to know so very well. He told them through parables and stories about shepherds and sheep and of his Father in heaven and how they should love one other and as he walked among them they listened intently to his every word.

One afternoon as Jesus was teaching near a small town two men approached him asking, "Are you the Jesus, the one that John said he was unfit to tie his shoes?"

Jesus stopped speaking and smiled at the two men at the reference to words that had been spoken long ago. "That is me," he answered.

"John is dead," the first one said. "Herod Antipas had him beheaded. He asked us to let you know if anything should befall him."

Nathanael could see that Jesus was obviously shaken. He looked up into the sky for a moment as if he was composing himself and then placed his hand on the man's shoulder. "I tell you, among those born of women; no one is greater than John."

Jesus went away for a few days leaving the twelve to care for themselves while he was away. Nathanael and Philip spoke a lot about John, telling them about some of the things he had done while they had been with him. "He was a great man," Nathanael added at last. "I wish now that I could have done something for him."

"You did, my friend," said Philip placing a hand on his shoulder. "You stood by him as long as anyone and he knew it."

"Yes, but if I had stayed then maybe this wouldn't have happened."

No one knew how to answer that question and so quietly began to settle down for the night each giving Nathanael plenty of room to grieve. Only Philip remained content on being quiet and letting his friend think back on the times that he and John had been together. He sat for hours near the fire watching the yellow flames rise and fall and tiny sparks explode now and again.

"You know Philip," he said sadly. "We are so like these little twigs that are once alive and growing and then like these, in a snap are dead and being consumed. Life is so short and then it is over." He paused for a moment, thinking about the fire and then added. "I wonder where we are in our lives."

Once Jesus returned the next day he took them down to Jericho and stayed in the city for some time. He wanted to go up into the hills and pray and so he left them for some time while they did their best to find food and drink. After a few days, he returned looking refreshed to Nathanael and he gathered up the twelve and told them that they were going to go to Jerusalem.

It was a strange request for it seemed that the Jewish leaders were making trouble for him there but they shrugged it off as another of his ways and gathered their gear. As they walked along the dusty road leading out of Jericho Nathanael noticed a wrinkled, dusty, sunbaked blind man who was sitting on the outskirts of the town begging near the main road where they were heading for Jerusalem. Nathanael had been talking to Levi about Jerusalem, who had lived on the outskirts of the city before moving to Bethsaida where he had run into Jesus. Levi was telling Nathanael about how he had gotten started in the tax collection business when they suddenly heard the beggar's voice shouting.

"Son of David, have pity on me," he yelled moving his head back and forth as if he were looking for Jesus, his scabbed-over eyes seeing nothing. "Son of David," he yelled again even louder, "Have pity on me."

They had both stopped and were now looking to Jesus who was two or three strides past the man and was talking to Andrew and Peter and had thus far had ignored his pleads. "Should we tell him to be quiet?" asked Nathanael quietly as he began to grow weary of the constant yelling.

"No, just ignore him, our master has and so let's move on," suggested Levi noticing how far Jesus had moved away from them.

Then suddenly and unexpectedly Jesus stopped and turned around. Nathanael saw his face which seemed to be filled with concern and watched his eyes which bore right to the beggar on the side of the road. "Bring him to me," he commanded holding out his hand to the man as if he were able to pull the man to himself.

Nathanael looked at Levi whose eyes darted back to Jesus and then to his. "Let's go get him," he said then walked over to the man. They both grabbed an arm and lifted him quickly to his feet. He was much lighter than Nathanael would have thought he would be and as he came up he wasn't very steady and needed holding tightly as they half-dragged him to Jesus. All the while Jesus spoke quietly to Peter about something.

"I wonder how he knew that this was Jesus," Levi asked but being how Nathanael had no idea he said nothing else. It was also strange to him that the man called out to Jesus even though he was blind.

"What do you want of me," asked Jesus as they brought the man near to where he and Andrew and Peter had been speaking. The others were quietly watching in suspense as to what Jesus was going to do.

No matter how many times Nathanael had watched Jesus heal someone he was still in awe after the person had received what they had asked for. And it seemed that Jesus never healed the same way twice. Sometimes he held the person in his arms, sometimes he touched the person on the location that needed healing, and he remembered one time that Jesus mixed his saliva in the dirt to make a mud solution to place over a man's eye so that he could see. So this time he waited and watched intently as he did always.

"Master," the man responded meekly. "I want to see."

Jesus, almost sadly it seemed to Nathanael relaxed his shoulders and sighed. "Go your way; your faith has saved you."

The eyes blinked. That's all Nathanael saw him do, was blink. Before there was nothing but two half holes with old scabs covering them and now amazingly there were two healthy eyes blinking. And Jesus had done nothing but tell him to go on. He didn't say anything else, or touch them or spit on them, he just told him to go on his way.

The beggar couldn't believe what had happened. His eyes darting one direction and then the other, trying to take in everything that he hadn't been able to see before. He was so giddy that he couldn't stop laughing as he dropped to his knees thanking Jesus over and over again. Jesus touched his head lightly and told him to get up. And when he did, Jesus turned back down the road and began his discussion again with Peter and Andrew as if nothing had happened.

"How does he do that?" asked Nathanael curiously as they began again walking away from the town. The beggar was walking close to them but paid them no mind. Nathanael wondered what he would do now that he could no longer beg now that his sight had been cured. But he was just one more in a multitude of lost souls who had been either cured or brought to believe in something better than they had by this man Jesus.

"I don't know," answered Levi shaking his head as if he too was confused. "I have seen him do this a hundred times but still can't believe it when it happens. I know it is a gift from God but it's still something that doesn't seem to be possible. It was like when we saw him walking on water. How in the world did he do that? Who is this man?"

Nathanael wondered the same thing. Jesus was obviously a man of God, as no one else in the world could ever do these things without having the power of God with him. But these things he did were beyond Godly, they were unbelievable. And Jesus did them as if they were nothing. He never celebrated a miracle or told others about it. In fact, he typically told those who were healed to not tell anyone. What good did it do to perform a miracle if no one knew it, he wondered?

They walked together mostly in quiet thinking of these things they had talked about and wondering what he would do next. It was a long two-day walk into the mountains to get to Jerusalem and he was tired. They seemed to always be moving from one town to another, rising early and staying up until late. And then there were the healings. They would come into a town and the people would be lined up waiting for him for somehow they will have heard that he was coming. They came seeking him; the crippled, the blind, the mute, and the dying; all in expectation of being healed even though they could not explain why he could do so. They were all there at every town, more than Nathanael ever dreamed of being on the earth. And he healed them all.

"What do you think is going to happen when we get to Jerusalem," asked Levi after some silence between them.

"I'm not sure," said Nathanael. "He seems to suggest that something will happen but he's never really clear about anything he tells us. For some reason, he thinks the Pharisees are against him. I don't know why, although I remember when a group came to see John one day at the river and they were very annoyed with him for what he had been saying. But Jesus has never said the type of things John has said. I don't know why they would want to harm him at all."

"Yes, but he attracts many who are against the Romans and that is why I am afraid they will something to him to stop him."

Nathanael looked surprised. "The Romans?" he asked. "Are you afraid of the Romans?"

"Well, I'm not afraid of the Pharisees. I don't think they will do anything. What do they care? If we get into the trouble it will be with the Romans, won't it?"

"Well I'm not sure one way or the other," said Nathanael. "Romans or Pharisees, I doubt either will come between us. What in the world could they have against our Lord? He only makes other people's lives better. I've never seen a more peaceful loving person in my life."

"Me either, but don't you think all this talk about being the son of God might infuriate the hierarchy? At first, he rarely said anything but lately, he's been saying a lot. Won't that upset them when he says that he and God are one?"

Nathanael thought about this for a while without answering. He had seen Jesus walk on water and had seen him heal hundreds of people, but still he wasn't so sure who he was. Was he the son of God, Nathanael wondered? Could he be the one who he said he was? It was one thing to say that God sent you and altogether something different to hear him say that he is his son.

"You know I don't know," he muttered unconvinced. "So much has happened in the last year. Sometimes he's so kind and caring but then often he can be so aloof." He paused for a moment, thinking back when he was with John. "You know John wasn't like that. He was always the same. There was nothing he cared to do but to dunk those who needed salvation. Jesus, on the other hand, is all over the place. One moment he is a healer, the next he is a preacher, and now you are calling him the messiah."

"Well what would you call him?" he asked.

And Nathanael couldn't answer. Instead, he said nothing and they continued following the other disciples along the hard climb towards Jerusalem. He watched Jesus talking to the others and wondered what they were saying. Jesus rarely spoke to him except when he needed something done but Nathanael still felt that he cared for him. It was many of the contradictions he seemed to have, this man who nothing seemed to bother.

That evening they sat around a large fire that Judas had built. He had also bought some bread, figs, and beer. The beer was a little too stout but Nathanael drank it with the others. He would have preferred some wine but it would have been too expensive for that many people. The fire was warm and bright against the dark silhouettes around him. He ate the last piece of bread on his lap and laid his back against the ground. As it was with most evenings, he was tired and was hoping to get some sleep.

"Teacher," John said after a few moments of silence. "We saw someone driving out demons in your name, and we discussed among ourselves if we should prevent them because he does not follow us. What should we have done?"

Nathanael remembered seeing John and Andrew talking to a man who had been praying over a boy. Afterward, John had told them that a demon had been living in the boy for some time and the man was trying to get it out. Nathanael had seen Jesus do this many times but he had never been able to do it. In fact, he had never been able to do any healing except to make a fever go away in a little girl. Some of the Apostles like Peter and James had done many miracles but even they had no idea how they had done them.

Jesus looked around at all of them. "Do not prevent them," he said. "There is no one who performs a mighty deed in my name who can at the same time speak ill of me." He paused to let that sink in. It surprised Nathanael for he was sure Jesus was going to tell them to stop the man. If others were going about healing people then why couldn't they?

"I tell you for whoever is not against us, is for us. Anyone who gives you a cup of water to drink because you belong to Christ, amen, I say to you, he will surely not lose his reward."

It made some sense but was still confusing. Then again, most everything he said was confusing. The other day they had been walking and Jesus stopped to look at a fig tree but there was no fruit on it. He said a few words that Nathanael didn't hear and then walked off. The next day as they walked by the tree again it was withered to its roots. Peter pointed it out and Jesus said, "Amen I say to you, whoever says to this mountain, 'Be lifted up and thrown into the sea,' and does not doubt in his heart but believes that what he says will happen, it shall be done for him."

They had been lost completely on that point. What did he mean that we could throw a mountain into the sea?" asked Philip to Nathanael the next day as they walked far behind Jesus.

Nathanael just shook his head. "What does any of it mean?" he asked. "What are we doing following him, and for what purpose? He heals and we watch and he preaches and we listen and that's what we do every day. I'm not so sure what it is that he expects of us."

"Me neither," Philip agreed. "Maybe once we get to Jerusalem and go to the temple we shall know more. Surely the high priests will welcome us and then maybe we will understand."

The walk up the mountain to Jerusalem was getting harder. Nathanael thought they would never make it as the road seemed to wind back and forth until he was sure they had been on the same stretch before and were going nowhere. Philip who had taken this road many times before assured him that they were making progress and would be at the top before night. His tired battered feet begged him to stop but if Jesus who seemed to never rest could make it then he guessed he had too also.

"Where are we," he asked Philip as they drank from a well in a small town they had just entered.

"We're just east of Jerusalem," he answered looking around as if he were trying to remember if anything had changed since he had last been there. "It's called Bethany, but there's not much here."

"Well, I hope we can stay here for the night. I am worn out."

Suddenly Nathanael heard his name being called. "It's Jesus," called John who had been in front of them but well behind Jesus. "He wants to see you two."

Nathanael looked at Philip intently for a few seconds and then shrugged his shoulders. "I guess we better go up there and see what he wants."

When they arrived Jesus was sitting on a stone wall speaking to Peter as he often did. He looked up as Nathanael and Philip wove through the bodies to get to his side. "Go into the village opposite you, and immediately on entering, you will find a colt tethered on which no one has ever sat. Untie it and bring it here."

Instantly, a thousand questions sprang up in Nathanael's head. He wanted to ask how he knew it would be there and how in the world would anyone know that it had never been ridden before, but instead he asked no questions but glanced up at Peter to see what he thought, but Peter just shrugged. Then Nathanael nodded and hoped that Philip was listening intently to the instructions.

Then Jesus continued. "If anyone should say to you, 'Why are you doing this?' reply, 'The master has need of it and when finished will send it back here at once.'"

Nathanael glanced at Philip to see if he was going to ask any questions but his lips were shut as tight as his. Jesus had already turned back to Peter leaving them to figure it out and so Nathanael pointed to the village on the opposite side of the road. "I guess that is where he wants us to go," he said more to himself than to Philip.

Philip raised his eyebrows and shrugged his shoulders as if he had no better suggestion. "How will we know which colt it is that we are to get?" he asked once they entered into the village.

"I don't know," complained Nathanael. "Maybe there will only be one tethered?" he speculated.

Just then Nathanael stopped in his tracks. "Look Philip, a colt." He said this in disbelief for sure enough just as Jesus had predicted a few hundred feet in front of them tied to a gate was a colt.

"Do you reckon that is the one he was talking about?" Philip quickly asked.

"We will find out I guess," Nathanael answered as he began to walk cautiously over to the animal. "I don't see any others do you?"

The colt was carrying nothing, was youthful looking and was white all over with no blemishes anywhere that Nathanael could see. "How do we know if anyone has ever sat on it?" he asked naively.

"I'm not sure but I don't see any other colts around so let's untie it and take it back to the teacher. Maybe he can tell." Nathanael nodded and quickly untied the rope attached to the gate.

"What are you doing untying my colt," asked a man walking up behind Philip. He was carrying some small pelts in his arms. The man who was not very tall none the less had a rugged look and massive shoulders. He could have easily manhandled both of them if need be.

Nathanael froze as if he had been caught doing something bad and having no idea what to say nodded to Philip to say something. "We were told to come here and get this colt," he said self-consciously but trying his best to sound confident. "Our master told us to tell the owner that he was in need of it and that we would bring it back here once we were finished with it."

The man's brows were raised high as if he was confused. He looked at the colt and then back at the two men who were standing next to it. "Well as long as you bring it back. I've just got it from the flock and haven't even had a chance to ride it, so be careful, he might try and buck you."

Nathanael couldn't believe the man was just going to let them take the animal but was joyful to hear that no one had ever ridden it before. "How lucky was that," he said, "telling us he hadn't ridden it before?" Philip said nothing but kept glancing back towards the owner as they led the colt through the street. "For a moment I thought he was going to grab the reins from me."

"Yea, well you know what I was thinking all along back there?"

"What," asked Nathanael trying not to sound over anxious?

Philip grabbed the reins from Nathanael to stop him pausing for a moment as if to gather his thoughts. "Nathanael, how did he know? How did he know the colt would be there, and how did he know that it would be tied to a gate, and how did he know that it had never been ridden on, and lastly, how did he know that the stranger would give it to us?"

Nathanael took back the reins and began walking again. "I have no idea Philip. He seems to be able to see into the future or something like that. To tell you the truth it's a little scary."

"It's more than scary Nathanael. This is really strange."

Nathanael didn't have to reply. He shook his head as if he was totally confused but deep inside he knew that Philip had guessed exactly what he had been thinking. Walking on water, healing cripples and blind people, multiplying fishes and loaves to feed people and now knowing what was going to happen before it happened. Yes, this was very strange, he thought as they spotted

Jesus standing where he had been before. He looked up at them as the approached and smiled as he saw the colt.

Chapter 14 – Jerusalem

Antipas had gone to drinking very heavily to ease his headaches after seeing the head of his friend on the platter, but it didn't really help. The next day after the beheading he decided to go back to Tiberius and stopped along the way at the river crossing. After getting off his horse he walked down to the water which had been empty of people since the arrest of John. Manaen was at his side as he knelt down and placed his hand in the water.

"Why did she do that," he asked more to himself than to his friend? "Why did she have to go that far?"

Manaen said nothing. There were times to speak up and there were times to remain quiet and he knew that this was a time to let Antipas vet his feelings without interruption. The crisp water was cold on his fingers as he tried to imagine his friend standing in the middle in his camel skin shirt looking up at him, his tired deeply sunk eyes none-the-less sparkling with life. What gave him that joy, he wondered? What made him spend countless hours every day up to his waist in all types of weather calling people to a non-existent god?

"Manaen, do you think there is a God?" he asked his old friend.

Manaen shook his head up and down. "Yes, my Lord," he answered taken somewhat aback by the question. "He is the God of our forefathers; Abraham and Moses."

"Yes, I know that," Antipas said in return as he stood watching the water run by. "But is there really a God?" he asked. "Will God punish me for cutting off his head for Herodias?

Manaen didn't know what to say in answer to that question. Who knew what God did or didn't do he thought. "I am sure that he will be lenient, my Lord after all you are his chosen one whom he put on his throne."

Antipas grinned. "So was Saul, and looked what happened to him."

Manaen knew what Antipas was referring to. Saul had been the first king chosen by God to lead his people and he had been overthrown by David after having disobeyed him. It was an unfair comparison he thought for Saul was half-crazy with jealousy of David to begin with. "You are a much more compassionate ruler than Saul was my Lord," he said knowing very well that it would not appease him.

Antipas was still thinking of John's head sitting on the platter with his eyes wide open. He couldn't get that picture out of his mind. Every night since that day he had awakened to a dream about cutting off someone's head, including Herodias. "But then don't forget what happened to Jehoiachin when the Babylonians came," Antipas said half-heartedly. "I don't recall God helping him out either."

"My Lord, I don't think this kind of talk is very healthy. Why don't we go on to Tiberius? You are so much happier there."

Antipas agreed and lifted himself up onto his horse. He looked one last time out over the river trying to imagine his friend saying farewell. "I will miss him Manaen. He was a good man, you know. He didn't deserve to die that way."

"Yes, Lord. Now let's go on. We should be home in a couple of days."

Immediately upon arriving in Tiberius Antipas found that he had received a letter from Pontius Pilate addressed to him. Antipas poured a strong cup of wine and walked out onto the cool terrace to read it. It read very simply;

COME TO JERSUSALEM. I WOULD LIKE TO DISCUSS SOME THINGS. PILATE

It was typical of Pilate to not say any more than he had but being how Antipas was alone in Tiberius and didn't expect Herodias to come to him anytime in the foreseeable future, he decided to go to Jerusalem and visit with him. There was plenty to do here, he thought but reckoned it wouldn't hurt to get away from his kingdom for a while and hopefully forget about John. So Antipas put Manaen in charge of putting a small caravan together with enough clothes for him to stay comfortably for a month if needed. Then he wrote a quick note back to Pilate saying he would be there in a week and sent it that very night to Jerusalem.

Antipas had decided to take the river road that followed the Jordon from the Sea of Galilee and then cut over to Jericho and up to Jerusalem. It might take him a day longer but it was well traveled and gave them ample supply of water and fresh dates that grew along the road. Besides, he would once again be able to stop and see the spot where John had baptized.

Two days later and after a long visit at the river they had left Jericho well behind and were approaching Jerusalem when the convoy suddenly stopped. "What is going on," he yelled towards his commander of his guard. "Go up ahead and find out what is the holdup."

After what seemed like an eternity, the guard made his way back to where Antipas sat impatiently waiting on his horse. "It seems that there is a vast crowd up ahead blocking the road," he said in reply, bowing his head as he did so. "It doesn't seem to be anything more than a lot of people listening to some man speak."

Antipas grunted his displeasure as he nudged his horse between the guard's horses and then the baggage carriers. Manaen followed closely as well as the commander of the guards weaving between the members of Antipas' household until they finally broke free of their caravan and saw the crowds before them. Antipas immediately spotted a man robed in white standing along the edge of the road speaking to the crowds that were surrounding him and they all seemed to be hanging on to his every word.

"Get out of my way," he suddenly shouted from atop his horse which caused the animal to throw his head back and prance briefly in surprise at the booming voice. Everyone turned to see Antipas looking magnificent upon his black horse with his sword drawn waving it through the air and looking as if he would use it, and immediately they began to move aside. "I said get out of the way," he shouted again even louder his left hand holding the reins tightly as he continued to swing the right with his sword.

They ducked and crushed against each other as panic set in but were unable to move very far because of the packed crowd on the road. Then suddenly a man squeezed through the crowd speaking as he came but not looking towards Antipas. Instead, he was speaking calmly to those who had been on the outside and had not been able to hear as well. The crowd still weary of the soldier on the horse none the less followed the man's every move and no one dared say a word while he continued to speak. He looked like any other man in the crowd to Antipas but he could not help but be intrigued by the way he spoke. It was as if he had a spell on everyone.

"There will be signs in the sun, the moon and the stars" Antipas heard him saying as he watched the man control the audience. His voice was soft but firm as he spoke slowly. "And on earth nations will be in dismay, perplexed by the roaring of the sea and the waves."

As he continued he easily turned so as to speak to everyone individually until he finally faced Antipas. He stared directly into his eyes as John had done many times. "People will die of fright in anticipation of what is coming upon the world," he continued as speaking just to Antipas and no one else. "For the powers of the heavens will be shaken."

The man then stopped speaking for a moment, his eyes still locked on Antipas' eyes as he let the words sink in. Then he began again as he continued slowly walking along but his eyes were still glued to Antipas. "And then they will see the Son of Man coming in a cloud with power and great glory." By now he had circled around so that he was again just a few feet from Antipas's horse but as before had never taken his eyes from him. "But when these signs begin to happen, stand erect and raise your heads because your redemption is at hand."

They stood there looking at each other, neither moving, neither saying a word and everyone watched. For the crowd knew who the king was, and they knew who this man was, and thus to them this was a defining moment between two different worlds; of God and of man.

But Antipas, although enamored with the words he had heard, would have no part in arguing with a common intenerate teacher. "If you don't ask this mob to move out and let us by," he said calmly but in loud commanding voice, "I will unleash my guards and they will indeed make a path through. Is that clear?"

The man showed no expression that Antipas could see. Instead, he moved towards the middle of the crowds and began teaching again while completely ignoring Antipas. "Consider the fig tree and all the other trees," he said as he circled through the crowds, his voice loud enough to be heard be Antipas. "When their buds burst open, you see for yourselves and know that summer is now near; in the same way, when you see these things happening, know that the kingdom of God is near."

Antipas was angry. "Who is this guy?" he asked Manaen leaning towards his friend in his saddle. "Do I know him?"

"I think he is the man they call the healer," he answered his voice low.

"Who," Antipas asked looking confused. "Is that supposed to mean something to me?"

"My Lord, if you think back you may remember that this man had passed through Tiberius a few months ago with a large crowd following, and one of your guards reported this to us. Since the man and his crowd had moved through without any disturbances and were gone even before it was reported to us, we ignored them. I believe he is that the same man; Jesus from Nazareth I believe they called him. He is some sort of healer."

206

Antipas thought back but couldn't remember the event. "And you may remember," Manaen continued, "the time that it was reported that someone had been raised after being dead for four days in Bethany. We scoffed at that also my Lord."

This time, Antipas did remember. They had all had a good laugh over that one but something had stuck in his head that took a while to get over; the number of people who had actually said they had seen the man Lazarus rise out of the tomb was staggering. Could they had all been under some kind of spell cast by this magician? And now, here he was, speaking in riddles of fig trees, buds bursting open, and God coming.

Then suddenly Antipas broke out in a sweat. This Jesus didn't look like John, but he sure sounded and acted just as he had. Antipas wanted to talk to him, wanted to ask him about Lazarus, wanted to see him heal someone, but before he had a chance the preacher/healer broke through the crowd way ahead of them and began to climb the road towards Jerusalem leaving him behind within the throng.

"Manaen," he said sweat running down his face and into his eyes and his lip now shaking profusely. "It is John," he said becoming sick at his stomach. "It is John whom I beheaded. He has been raised like the Lazarus fellow."

"My Lord," Manaen responded after a slight pause trying to understand his words. "Are you alright? John is dead."

Antipas did not answer nor did he really hear his friend. Instead, he immediately kicked his horse and took off after Jesus with Manaen quickly at his side. "My Lord is this wise?" he asked speaking as low as he could and still be heard. "I think we should go on to Jerusalem where you can rest."

"No, Manaen, you go on. I have got to talk to this man. I have to see if he is John."

It took some time to catch up to him while negotiating the rough road and pushing their steeds between the crowds following him, but finally Antipas came upon Jesus who was talking as he walked. Antipas had long ago sheathed his sword but he was still weary of the crowd for this man spoke of things that were not worldly, and that bothered him. He rode alongside him for a time waiting for Jesus to stop talking and recognize that he was there, but soon he realized that he was not going to do so and this irritated Antipas even more.

"Will you speak to me?" he asked abruptly as he nudged his horse into Jesus' side jostling him into several others.

Jesus gathered his balance and turned to look up at Antipas. He said nothing but just stared and Antipas wondered if he was doing that on purpose or if he really had nothing to say. The longer he said nothing the angrier Antipas got until finally, he yelled. "For crying out loud, will you say something?"

Jesus smiled slightly as he searched his face and then finally answered. "What do you want me to say?" he began slowly but succinctly his eyes now bearing up into Antipas. "That you are the murderer of John and that you and your wife Herodias are living in sin and that on the last day when the Son of Man comes back from the dead, your life will be required of you?"

Antipas' jaw dropped for he had no clue these words would come out of his mouth. Jesus stood tall and confident daring the once proud Antipas to contradict him. But there were no words coming forth from Antipas' mouth, all he could do was to sit on his horse and stare back. Then without warning, Jesus turned back to his companion whom he had been speaking to and began to walk as they continued their conversation again.

Antipas did not move. Instead, he sat silently staring in disbelief at the back of the stranger and watched him as he easily and gracefully continued walking and speaking to others as if nothing had happened. Was he really John he wondered; coming back to haunt him for what he had done. Then he shook his head as if to regain his composure.

"Why is everyone so concerned about my marriage," he shouted loudly spooking his horse and all those around him. But the man he had said this for had moved quite a ways up the road and did not turn back.

"Manaen," Antipas almost shouted. "Let us get moving again. We have wasted too much time here."

Manaen kicked his horse sharply in the side to get the large animal to move but his mind was on nothing but the man whom Antipas thought was John. He watched his friend Antipas as he turned away from the crowd and began to ride with his head cast down and shoulders slumped over. Two men, he thought to himself. Two men who seemed to be completely unconnected, both who had touched something inside his friend that was killing him, and no one else in the world could have spoken as they had to him. Who were these men and what power did they have over others?

Antipas thought of little else as he rode into Jerusalem. Had God been playing tricks on him? Had he really brought John back in another man's body so as to further torment him? He was beginning to dread having married Herodias and certainly having bowed down to her request for John's head. And at that moment, he regretted having come to Jerusalem to see Pilate. He had even thought of turning back to Tiberius but worried what his people might think. There was nothing right now that could possibly ease his mind of all these thoughts.

Jerusalem looked the same as it always did; it's large stone walls looking formidable sitting upon the apex of the mountain, with its cream-colored stone buildings rising above them. It had been the most beautiful city in the world Antipas had once thought until he had gone to Rome, which put every city to shame. Nothing could compare to the capital of the empire although Jerusalem was beautiful and majestic in her own right. He couldn't imagine even Rome taking this city in a battle although he knew that they had conquered equally impressive fortresses like Carthage and Alexandria.

But these were different times and hopefully peaceful times except for a few rebel rousers that caused problems now and then. But then that was why they had sent Pilate, to quell such groups. Thankfully there was nothing going on now as he entered the city and began his ascent past Pilates' citadel. He would spend a few quiet weeks here and then go home and get away from everyone who had been causing him headaches.

Antipas tried his best to sneak quietly into his own palace along the eastern wall of Jerusalem but no sooner had he entered his palace walls then there was a greeting from a centurion with a message from Pilate. Antipas was to meet Pilate for dinner in the Antonia Fortress that evening. Antipas sighed but sent back a message that he would be there. But first, he wanted a bath more than anything after the long hard dirty ride.

"Antipas," exclaimed Pilate from across the room where he was reclining on a sofa. Standing he greeted him like a forgotten brother from long ago. "How I have missed your company," he exclaimed slapping him on the back. "Come sit and have some wine with me. Dinner will be served in a bit."

Antipas drank heartily throwing down three full cups of wine, one after another. Pilate barely drank and watched through amused eyes. "Thirsty old friend," he said as the third cup went down.

Antipas suddenly felt embarrassed. "It was a long hard ride. My backend hurts and I have not had a decent wine in days." He held out his cup to the steward for another pour. "But thank you for asking."

Pilate laughed. "You know, things have been getting a bit rowdy here as late and that is why I have decided to stay for a while. It is not a cool as in Caesarea but the climate is dry and I can stomach the smell." He paused for a moment to drink some of his wine and when Antipas said nothing, he continued. "I have been hearing a lot about this man Jesus as of late."

Antipas who had been ignoring Pilate's gaze suddenly looked up. "Jesus?" he said stammering.

Pilate was intrigued for he had no idea if Antipas had ever confronted this man who had been stirring up the Jewish hierarchy. He waited a moment but received no other reaction from his friend. "I understand that he was an associate of your John, who If I recall I saw lose his head at your birthday party. Do you know of him?"

Antipas looked down at his sandaled feet and took a deep breath. "Yes, I think I met him."

Pilate suddenly rose from his reclining position throwing his feet onto the ground and leaned at Antipas in anticipation. "You have?" he asked excitedly. "Where did you meet him?"

Antipas looked surprised. "Why just today. I passed him somewhere before reaching Bethany. He was being followed by a large crowd. I'm surprised you haven't heard."

Pilate hadn't heard and that infuriated him to no end, but he didn't lead on that he hadn't. "What did he look like?" he asked still leaning forward in anticipation of being told something of utmost importance.

Antipas thought back to earlier that day but couldn't quite capture his features. "Well, I'm not really sure," he said. "I was on my horse and he was walking. He had a white robe and all though he was plain enough looking he appeared to be a little taller than the others. His hair was long and dark and if I am remembering correctly he had a full beard."

"What did he say," interrupted Pilate.

Antipas looked up but Pilate could tell from his eyes that he was in a far off place. "He commented about my marriage," he answered slowly as if in deep thought. "Why does everyone have something to say about my marriage?"

"And what did you say back?" he asked becoming impatient and less intrigued with Antipas by the moment for his answers were not very coherent.

"Why I'm not sure. But whatever I said did not make an impact for he completely ignored me. Can you believe that " he said staring into his wine? "He completely ignored his king?"

Pilate could tell that Antipas was shaken about something and that to ask any further questions was pointless. "Well, maybe you need to get some rest. We can talk again once you've had a chance to get comfortable in your palace. I will call on you within the week."

Antipas nodded and rose to leave but then stopped. He turned and looked at Pilate intently. "You know I thought that he was John, who had come back to haunt me."

Pilate laughed and patted Antipas on his back as he escorted him to the door. "You go get some rest. We will speak of this later."

Pilate shook his head as he watched Antipas walk through the main doors leading into the street. "I wonder what this Jesus said to shake him up so much?" he asked himself then turned to go back to his dinner.

Herod's palace had been built by his father a long time ago. It was the largest home in the walls of Jerusalem but stayed empty much of the time now that Antipas' half-brother had died and the

Roman's had taken over. It remained empty except for a hand full of servants who stayed in waiting just in case Antipas showed up, so he was relieved to have people waiting on him when he came in. Although he had not eaten anything at Pilate's he went straight into his bedroom and collapsed on his bed where he stayed for two straight days.

It was a servant who had finally woke him saying that an important message had just been delivered from Pilate. Antipas rolled out of bed noting that it was still very early in the morning and wondering what the urgency at this time of day would be. Trudging through the courtyard he entered his office and there before him was a note staring at him on a silver tray on his desk. It read holding the letter up to a candle:

I AM SENDING YOU THE HEALER CALLED JESUS. THE JEWS WANT HIM CRUCIFIED BUT I CAN'T FIND ANYTHING FOR WHICH HE DID THAT WOULD WARRANT HAVING HIM KILLED. HE'S FROM YOUR PROVINCE OF GALILEE SO SEE WHAT YOU CAN DO TO PLACATE THEM – PILATE.

The words disturbed Antipas. Why in the world would the Jews want him crucified, he wondered? And Pilate's accusation that it was somehow his fault because this man came from Galilee was preposterous. If he couldn't get them off of Pilate's back then Pilate would blame him for an uprising in his province and there was no way for Antipas to argue against it.

"I should have arrested him on the road and sent him back to Tiberius," he said to himself. "Then I wouldn't be in this position."

Antipas put the note down and sighed. There was nothing he could do but see the man and so he went into his room and put on his military garb which he liked to wear when judging. It made him look official and usually intimidated the other side. But even as he was putting on his uniform he wondered what this man had done to upset the Jews so much. The thought that they would want to have him crucified was unthinkable. Why the man had been walking around the Galilee region for three years and had never caused any trouble at all as far as he knew. Then he remembered John. Antipas had made one mistake already by allowing John to be beheaded and it was already causing him immense grief. He didn't want to be the cause of having someone else's murder on his hands also.

Chapter 15 – Passover

As they left Bethany and began to descend the Mount of Olives, Nathanael became worried with the huge crowds honing in on them as Jesus made his way down the slopes sitting on the donkey. At first, Nathanael thought the use of a donkey somewhat pointless when they could just as easily obtained a horse or a cart, but Jesus insisted and so here he was riding bareback on this animal. The weird thing that Nathanael noticed and could not get over was that hundreds were waiting for Jesus and waving palms and shouting at him.

It was just three days before Passover and so, of course, Jerusalem would be crowded but the sight of this many people was disturbing. Throngs of them stood on each side of the road from the valley all the way up to the Golden Gate which would lead them into Jerusalem and to the Temple. And it was as if they knew he would be coming that led them to be all lined up to see him.

"Why are they shouting?" Nathanael yelled in order to have Philip hear him above the noise.

"I don't know," he shouted back. "But they obviously think he is someone. Look at the way they adore him. It's almost as if they thought that he was their liberator or something."

"That's crazy," answered Nathanael not understanding why anyone would think such a thing. After all, Jesus was harmless. He never carried a weapon, never cursed or struck anyone, and most of all never spoke once about liberating anyone from the Romans. In fact, Nathanael couldn't remember Jesus ever saying anything about the Romans at all, much less how to get rid of them.

And as they neared the gate he began to hear what they were saying. "Hosanna! Blessed is he who comes in the name of the Lord!" while others responded, "Blessed is the coming kingdom of our father David! Hosanna in the highest!" How odd, he thought and kept his eyes out for Romans.

After entering through the gate they went to a house that Jesus had already secured for them for Passover. It was a large spacious room on a second floor with a small terrace overlooking a public courtyard. He was relieved to get away from the crowds but even more so, the Romans. He never saw any soldiers in Galilee or Perea but they were everywhere here and it disturbed him. They always looked menacing and ready to take your head off if you looked at them wrong. He decided that from now on he would steer clear of them even if it meant going out of his way to do so.

Nathanael looked around the room eyeing his fellow apostles as they waited for Jesus to finish speaking to his mother. He had stopped her outside in the garden while the rest went up the steep flight of stairs and began sitting around the large wooden table in the middle of the room. It was a long table surrounded by stools and benches enough to sit the twelve. Nathanael sat on a bench next to his good friend Philip who sat staring at his feet which were calloused and thick with dust. He glanced at his own feet seeing something quite similar in his sandals. He couldn't remember when they had not been bruised and sore from all the walking they had done over the last few years.

Simon Peter, now known to everyone as Peter from the name Jesus gave him a few weeks earlier, stood leaning against the far wall. It was rare to see him relax as it was his nature to always be doing something. He could no more sit at the table and be still then an eagle could remain sitting on a tree limb as fish jumped all about the lake. Directly across from Nathanael was John, the youngest of the lot. He was shy and often sat alone but somehow had gotten a seat towards the middle of the table. His eyes never moved from their lowered position even as the others whispered or moved about.

The other Simon sat next to Judas to the right of Nathanael. Judas' eyes were always darting around as if looking to see if he was being watched. Nathanael didn't like him very much as he was a loner, like John, but not humble as the younger Apostle was. He seemed to always be arguing and wanting to begin something even if it meant getting arrested. Mathew sat next to James; one of Zebedee's sons, whom he liked very much but for some reason never spoke too much too, and to his left at the end of the table was Andrew. Andrew was also very likable and was well respected by all of the Apostles. He had a keen mind and never jumped into a matter unless he thought deeply first. On the other side of him wa Thomas, another quiet fellow who mostly followed the crowd an rarely got involved in their discussions. The other James rubbed sore arm muscle that he had hurt in a fall the day before an Thaddeus, who was whispering to him, rounded out the twelve.

When Jesus came in they all looked up at him. He strolled i quietly as if he didn't belong there but we knew he did. He carried presence about him that no one else could; someone who was leader but walked as if he was not. Nathanael watched his eye which greeted everyone individually with kindness and yet wit authority. Then he eased around to the other side of the table an began the Passover ritual as the sun dropped below the horizon.

"I have eagerly desired to eat this Passover with you before suffer," he began. "For I tell you, I shall not eat again until there i fulfillment in the kingdom of God."

Nathanael's eyes darted to Peter's who looked stupefiec This had not been the first time he had spoken about the coming o the kingdom but no one had understood what he had meant befor and had been afraid to ask. Within the last few weeks, he had said s many things that had been disturbing to all of them, especially t Nathanael. He had lost one very special friend in John and did nc want to lose another.

Then Jesus leaned over and picked up a cup full of wine. H gave thanks, and said, "Take this and share it among yourselves; fo

I tell that from this time on I shall not drink of the fruit of the vine until the kingdom of God comes."

There it was again. Did that mean that he wasn't going to drink anything again after tonight? What sort of talk was this Nathanael wondered? And how would they know that the Kingdom had come?

Then Nathanael watched Jesus set the cup down and pick up some bread. Again he blessed it, broke it, and gave each of them a piece, saying, "This is my body, which will be given for you; do this in memory of me."

Nathanael did what everyone else in the room was doing and placed the piece in his mouth and chewed on it. It tasted the same as every other Passover bread had ever tasted but this time, Jesus was telling them that this was his body they were eating. It did not make any sense but he said nothing in response to Jesus' words. Often Jesus got into one of those moods where he became mystical and said things that were sometimes very hard to understand. This was one of those times.

Then again Jesus picked up the cup and said, "This cup is the new covenant in my blood, which will be shed for you."

Nathanael again glanced around the room hoping to see someone else as confused as he was who might speak up and ask what he meant, but none did. Why did he say that he would be shedding his own blood?

Jesus ended with a psalm which he sang. It was beautiful and Nathanael again felt peaceful as he always did when he sang. It was a peace he had not had until he had begun to listen to Jesus and as he listened now he realized how fond he had grown of this man. He had walked Galilee with him ever since he had left John and that had been over two years ago. But lately, the things he was saying seemed to be about betrayers and conspiracies and death by the Jews. He had tried to talk with some of the others but no one knew what he was getting at and no one had the courage to ask.

After the Passover supper, Jesus had taken the twelve to the Mount of Olives, which he had done earlier. He liked the coolness and quietness of the place and so it seemed as it would be like another evening passed around the campfire. But after gathering near a large olive tree Jesus got very quiet. Nathanael could tell something was bothering him and that he wanted to tell them what it was.

"This night all of you will have your faith in me shaken, for it is written; 'I will strike the shepherd and the sheep of the flock will be dispersed.'"

Nathanael felt worried at these words. Here he again was talking of something wrong going to happen and it frightened him. "But after I have been raised up, I shall go before you to Galilee," he said.

Again eyes began shifting to one another looking for an answer but none was found until finally, Peter spoke up. "Master, though all may have their faith in you shaken, mine will never be."

Jesus put his hand on Peter's shoulder and smiled that half-smile he often used when teaching something. "Peter, I say to you, this very night before the cock crows, you will deny me three times."

Nathanael gulped. He was staring at Peter whose eyes were wide and fist clenched as he often did when he was riled up. "Even though I should have to die with you," he said with all the passion he could pour out to Jesus, "I will not deny you."

Then Andrew said the same thing and then James and John jumped in and said they would be with him and when Philip jumped up and agreed with Peter, Nathanael did likewise. Jesus looked at them sadly and lowered his head. He thought he saw a tear running down his master's face.

Twice during the night, Nathanael heard Jesus speaking to Peter but he was too tired to pay attention and immediately fell back to sleep. Then suddenly a foot slammed into his hip causing him to jump up as he looked around only to see a large contingent of Jewish guards, dressed in their military gear with their swords out and who were surrounding Jesus with Judas standing next to him his face looking empty as if he had no life left in him.

"Have you come out as against a robber, with swords and clubs to seize me?" Jesus exclaimed to the guards. "Day after day I sat teaching in the temple area, yet you did not arrest me."

Nathanael could see he was angry but did not have any idea what was happening or why. He moved next to Philip and nudged him. "What's going on?" he asked as softly as he could.

"I don't know," answered Philip equally as soft. "But I saw Judas kiss Jesus just before the guards came out. I think they may be trying to arrest him."

Then Jesus looked over to the apostles standing together away from the guards and he spoke to them. "But all of this has come to pass that the writings of the prophets may be fulfilled."

As he said this the temple guards grabbed him forcibly by the arms and began to drag him away. Several other guards pointed their swords at the apostles and stepped towards them as if they were going to harm them and that's when they began to run. Nathanael didn't understand why he was running, he just was and with him, everyone else was also. Finally, Peter stopped and held up his hand. "Wait," he said breathing hard. They had run a good distance and many had fallen and skimmed themselves. "We must find out where they are taking him," he shouted loudly and everyone looked up the hill to see if he had been heard.

"Not so loud," James said looking back at Peter. "What do you have in mind?"

"Some of us should follow him," he said half-heartedly.

"You go, Peter," said Andrew. "You're the one who said that you would never deny him."

Peter looked hurt. "OK, I will go. Anyone else wants to come with me?"

Everyone looked at each other but no one said a word. Then finally little John raised his hand. "I will go with you Peter," he said.

"Well we will go find out what in the world is happening and once we have I will send John back here to get you. We can't just let them take him away like that."

Peter did not sound very convincing to Nathanael and was about to say something when James jumped in. "But what can we do?" asked James. "We have no weapons and even if we did, none of us have ever used one."

"Yea," echoed Andrew. "What can we do?"

"I don't know but once we locate him I will figure something out. Now, find someplace to hide until we can get back with you."

"How about the house where we had Passover," Nathanael spouted out suddenly, not knowing why he had done so. He had been shaking ever since he had jumped up and seen the mob surrounding Jesus.

"Good idea, Nathanael," said Peter and then grabbed John by the arm. "We will try and see what is going on." Then he left them and headed back up through the olive grove.

They watched Peter and John disappear before locking themselves back in the upper room. Everyone looked worried as they waited for news but none came. As the day wore on James suggested that someone go out and try and find them something to eat but his words fell on deaf ears. Nathanael had no desire to go out into the streets with Jesus in chains and maybe now even Peter. If the Romans or the Jewish leaders found out where they were then they might all be arrested.

Chapter 16 – King Herod

Antipas's lip quivered so bad that it was all he could think about and along with it, he now had a severe burning sensation in his stomach. Herodias had always been quick to fix up an elixir of herbs to counteract his burning stomach but she wasn't here and he couldn't very well tell anyone else that his stomach hurt. What kind of king would whine about something like that to his subjects? He had been a wreck ever since he had had John beheaded, with stomach problems being the worst of his ailments. He had even been going to bed later and later and when he finally did sleep it was only to wake to nightmares of John causing him to get up and resort to drinking more wine.

His throne room was near the entrance to the palace gate that opened into the city center. He thanked God that his palace on the eastern wall was all the way across the City from Pilate's Antonia Fortress, so Jesus could be only half way there, or he might be just outside his gates depending on how fast the messenger had traveled and when Pilate had sent him. Antipas guessed that the procession through the city would be slow and he would have a long wait ahead of him and so he had one of his servants bring him a cup of wine hoping that it would soothe his stomach.

The wine didn't help his stomach at all but it did calm his nerves and eased his twitching lip. Not wanting to be alone with this man after having already having exchanged words on the road to Bethany, he sent word to his friend Manaen who now set in a chair near his but of course not on the dais which covered a large area in the center of the room. A fireplace covering a quarter of the northern wall sparkled red and gold with hot embers but did little to warm him. Instead, he had covered himself with a large black bear fur that broke the morning chill and he waited.

He was on his second cup of wine when suddenly the doors flew open and two guards entered followed by a man whose hands were chained to a pole that lay across the shoulders of two more armed guards, causing the accused to have to hold his arms perpetually up in the air. Antipas eyed the guards, who were obviously Pilate's men and nodded at them to drop the pole. When they did the man fell to his knees causing the chains to crash loudly against the tiled floor startling Antipas who had just gotten comfortable in his chair. Then after a short moment of getting his balance, the man looked up and stared at Antipas as he had on the road to Bethany.

Antipas did not like this man like he had liked John even though they had both told him the same thing. John was warm and friendly where this man was cold and his directness was unnerving. He hated that Pilate had sent him over for he had no desire to interrogate him. He wished he would just go away and leave him alone.

"So on the road, you didn't want to speak to me," he said harshly sitting up on his throne and leaning forward to be more kingly. No matter who or what this man claimed to be, he thought, he was the king and he was power and this man could do nothing but grovel if he wished to keep his life. "Now what have you to say for yourself?" he asked coldly.

He was quite prepared to lash out at anything the man tried to say on his own behalf but instead to Antipas' bewilderment, he said nothing. Instead, he just stared, his cold gray eyes burning into his. Antipas began to fidget with his robe and grew furious by the moment but had no idea what to do. It angered him that he could not make him speak.

"I said," he bellowed suddenly standing with his fist clenched and face reddened. It was as if his words were being spat from his mouth. "What do you have to say for yourself?"

But again the man said nothing, which infuriated Antipas even more. "What's the matter, healer," he said more calmly deciding on taking a different approach. "Have you nothing to say? You were more than willing to condemn me on the road to Bethany. How have things turned haven't they? Now you are here and I am most ready to condemn you for those horrible false statements you made about me." He paused for a moment waiting for any word but still got no reply.

"So what do you have to say about that son of God?" he said laughing. "You are the son of God, aren't you?"

Jesus' face remained steadfast, his sore muscles aching across his back. But he did nothing to allow Antipas to think he was in discomfort. Once again, he just stared, neither in anger nor in pity.

Antipas' laughter finally died out. His had been the only sound in the chamber, the guards having dared not even smile and suddenly realizing this he began to grow angry again. He glanced over at his friend Manaen seeking someone to befriend him. "Maybe he could show us a miracle, huh my friend? If he did a miracle for us then we would believe that he is the son of God, correct?"

Manaen said nothing for he did not like where this was heading so Antipas turned back to his prisoner. "So Jesus, you are a miracle worker and preacher, aren't you? Then if you are, why don't you perform a miracle for us?" He had quit laughing and his forced smile looked malevolent. "Tell me what would you like to do for us? Should I send one of the guards out to find a cripple for you to heal, or maybe a blind man so that you can make him see?"

To his utter amazement, Jesus said nothing but just kept staring at him, which was beginning to become unnerving. He wished at least he would look away. "Then I guess we must find something else to do." He was angry at having John killed, at his stomach hurting, at Pilate and Herodias and here was someone he could take it out on.

"Yes," he said as if he had just formulated a plan. "I have a better idea," he said his arms stretched out wide as he smiled. "How about healing yourself? Why don't I have you lashed and then you can heal your cuts. Now that would be all telling, wouldn't it mister son of God? What do you think Manaen? Wouldn't that be something to see?"

But Manaen said nothing. He didn't want to be any part of this man's torment and so he held his tongue tightly. Antipas' eyes darted over to Manaen but they didn't stay there long. "Well, are you going to show us a miracle or not?" he asked again, his voice now high and sounding uncontrollable. Then he finally screamed as loud as he could, "Make me a miracle, you liar."

He was breathing heavily now with sweat running down the side of his face and spittle all over his chin. It took all he could gather to calm his voice. "Either you are, or you are not the son of God," he explained his voice now very low but distinct. "And if you are not, as I assume you aren't, then that explains why it is that you can't perform any miracles."

But still, nothing was said. Antipas peered at him sharply waiting for something but got nothing. Then he threw his hands up in the air. "You're just a fraud," he yelled again. "That's what you are, a fraud."

Antipas spun towards his guards. "Beat him," he commanded harshly then turned back to his throne and sat looking away from Jesus. "I want to see him bleed," he said staring up towards the ceiling. Then as an afterthought, he turned back to Jesus who hadn't removed his gaze at all from Antipas. "Well, we shall see who won't speak, won't we."

His guards quickly began to beat Jesus with short whips that tore into his skin and made him bleed profusely. In the meantime Antipas yelled as the blows were struck; "Five, six, seven, eight, nine," he bellowed as he watched the lashes rip the skin exposing bone and spraying blood on his clothes and all over the tile. Suddenly Antipas noticed the blood pooling upon his tile floor and yelled, "Stop."

The guards moved back and Antipas slowly walked around Jesus surveying his damage. For the first time, Jesus' did not have his head up and was not looking at Antipas. Then unexpectedly he grabbed his hair with his fist and yanked his head back so that Jesus was looking into his face which was just an inch away from his. Antipas could smell his sweat and feel his breath on his face. "Now what do you have to say," he asked? "You worthless little man."

But Jesus said nothing. "Speak to me you piece of filth or I will have you lashed again," Antipas shouted directly in his face.

But again there was no reply and so Antipas shoved Jesus' head down towards his feet then turned away and went back to his throne. Just as he plopped down on the seat he saw Jesus lift his head so that he could lock his eyes once again on Antipas. As he did this suddenly Antipas had a vision of John's head on that bloodied plate with his eyes open wide staring at him, and he shut his and screamed, "Will you not talk to me?"

When he opened them Jesus remained as he was, bleeding, in pain, but with his eyes still bearing down upon Antipas which caused him to sigh loudly and turned his head to look elsewhere. This man was obviously not going to say a word and what was he supposed to do if the man wouldn't even talk under the lash? He looked back down at the blood-splattered cloak and suddenly had an idea. If he couldn't make him talk, he would send him back to Pilate dressed as a king.

"My purple robe, quickly," he shouted to his guards. "And my red cape," he added excitedly, almost giggling. "Get me my red cape."

Antipas watched as his guards pulled the robe over Jesus' head and then placed the cape over his shoulders. He even laughed as they turned him around so that he could see. "Aw yes," he said. "That is lovely. How could Pilate not like him now Manaen," he said still laughing as he looked over at his friend. "I am sending him the king of the Jews."

"Now off with him," he said to the guards in a more normal tone. "I don't want to see him again. Take him back to Pilate tell him that I also see nothing here that is worthy of this man's death."

It had taken everything out of him. Antipas once again lay on his bed, his stomach burning his head aching and all alone. How could this man not say even a word in his on defense he wondered? Did he not care? Did he want to die? Antipas rolled over and took another swig of his wine but it did not help. It was a crisp clear night but even that did not make him feel any better. If only he could get some sleep.

The next morning it was the Sabbath but that did not prevent Pilate from sending a messenger with a note that he was coming over. Antipas had no desire to speak to him but there was nothing he could do to stop him and so he put on his finest white robe and sandals and waited for him on the open porch. The weather was still the same which made Jerusalem bearable and a nice breeze kept the smells of the city away. Even his stomach felt calmer after a rare good night's rest.

Pilate came in laughing. "I want to congratulate you, my friend," he said coming over to Antipas and slapping him on both his arms.

"And why am I being congratulated for?" he asked surprised at the friendliness of the visit.

"It was how you sent Jesus back to me," he said now smiling. "The purple robe and cape. It was perfect. It took everything in me to not start laughing. I still can't believe you did that."

Antipas smiled back. It was the first time in weeks that he had genuinely smiled at a comment. "Well, I thought I needed to do something after not getting anything out of him."

"You too? I barely got anything out of him. He was a strange person. It was like he didn't really care what I did with him."

"Same here," said Antipas in reply. "I expected him to at least say something but during the entire time that he was here, he said nothing. Absolutely nothing. That's when I got the idea to send him back as the king of the Jews."

Pilate laughed again. "Well Tetrarch, you made my day."

It was the first time that Pilate had ever used his title and that surprised Antipas. "Have a seat and I can send up for some bread and honey."

"That sounds perfect," he replied. "I'm famished."

"By the way," asked Antipas, "What happened to him? Did you let him go?"

Pilate shook his head. "No," he replied somewhat sadly. "Caiaphas pressured me into having him crucified."

Antipas' jaw dropped. "Crucified?" he asked. "For what?"

"Well at first Caiaphas argued that Jesus had blasphemed against the Jews for different things he had said and done."

"A bit harsh punishment for a squabble over religion," Antipas argued.

"Well, that's exactly what I told them. But then he tried to insist that this Jesus claimed to be the son of God. That's when I scoffed at them and sent him over to you. If they wanted to judge a religious point, then do it in front of their own king."

The use of his title emboldened him and for the first time felt important with Pilate. "Yea, I heard the same argument."

"But when they brought him back the fox had switched tactics. This time, they said that he was a revolutionary. That changed everything and he knew he had me. I asked him what he had done and they rattled off all sorts of charges about how he had discredited Caesar and the empire and that he had even gone as far as saying that he was a king."

"But did he really do those things," asked Antipas who was beginning to feel as if Pilate had been used so that the Jews could get what they wanted. But what was it that they really wanted, he wondered?

"I asked him and he said something trivial and so I had him scourged." He placed another piece of bread in the honey and shoved it in his mouth and followed it with a drink from his cup. "You know this is a very fine wine. I will have to get my steward to get some from you."

Antipas' eyes widened. "I believe that is my vintage," he remarked proudly. "I sent you over about fifty stone jars a few weeks ago."

"Are you sure," he asked taking another sip.

Antipas smiled. "I know my wine and this is mine."

"Well, then you have made my day. You surprise me my friend. That's twice in one day that you have impressed me. I will have my steward speak to yours and will make sure we have regular shipments."

"Thank you, Prefect."

"No, thank you for introducing me to this fine vintage," he said bowing his head slightly.

Antipas could not say anything he was so shocked at Pilate's friendliness. He watched him take one more drink before he continued. "Anyway, back to what's his name, Jesus. Ah yes, now where was I? So I still didn't think that was enough to have him killed, and so instead I had him scourged. I must say that my guard did a good job for he was bloodied from head to toe when they were through. There were pieces of meat and blood all over the floor."

Antipas winced at the thought and took a sip of wine to keep his stomach under control. "And then?" he asked in order to change the subject.

"Well, Caiaphas was very insistent that this man was a revolutionary and that if I didn't crucify him that they didn't know if they could prevent an uprising from the crowd and that might get back to Caesar and so on and so on. It was getting late, I was hungry, and I had had enough and so I finally gave in."

"That's too bad," said Antipas truly struck by the news. Yes he had been rough with him also, he was known for that, but he surely didn't feel the man should have been killed. "Caiaphas is usually not that hard with common criminals."

"It wasn't the revolutionary thing," explained Pilate. "It was the son of God thing. I could tell early on that he was incensed over some of the things this man had said about being the same as God. But to tell you the truth, I think it was the stunt with the donkey that might have been the final straw."

"What donkey stunt?" Antipas asked curiously. "I don't think I heard of it."

Pilate laughed. "You didn't see him ride into Jerusalem on an ass?" he exclaimed laughing. "Why people were in the streets with palm branches waving him on and yelling at him as if he were a king. I had my men keep an eye on him until we decided that he meant no harm. But I could tell that Caiaphas was really annoyed by it."

"Why?" asked Antipas. "What harm had he done? All I ever heard was that he was some sort of miracle worker. In fact, I told him I would let him go if he healed someone for me, but of course, he couldn't, or wouldn't."

Pilate laughed again. "My dear Antipas, you are a real hoot. The more you tell me, the more you make me laugh."

Antipas chuckled but really didn't mean it. "Well, it is ashamed that he had to be crucified. Why didn't they just stone him?"

"No, that would not have made their point. He wanted Jesus crucified from the very start. He wanted to make a point and he wanted Rome to make it."

"Well maybe now things will settle down."

"I hope so for your sake. Both this Jesus and John came from your provinces and Caesar will not like this type of thing to keep coming up again and again."

They spoke for some time then finally Pilate excused himself. After he had left Antipas strolled along the parapet looking over the grand city and thought back upon those two men that he had helped killed. Neither was his fault, he told himself. It was Herodias that wanted John beheaded and Caiaphas that had wanted

Jesus crucified. He was just a pawn, not a player. But the thing that bothered him the most, as he looked at the temple standing so high above all else, was why they had both received such harsh deaths. One had been beheaded and the other crucified. And it seemed that neither one had deserved it.

It was late in Jerusalem but there were still many fires and candles lit throughout. He wondered if anyone else cared about Jesus' death or for that matter John's. Looking up at the stars he wondered if and how they had been connected.

"I will go home tomorrow," he said out loud to no one. "It is finished, and I will no longer be bothered by either of these men."

Chapter 17 – Thomas

Peter did not come back that evening and so they huddled and waited only speaking occasionally to speculate as to what was happening. Several times they heard a dog bark and each time it happened they all jumped as if they were being attacked. James tried to laugh the first time but no one joined him. The second time they all smiled at each other but no one said a thing.

Nathanael woke to sunlight streaming in through a crack in the door that bore into his eyes. Everyone else was sleeping when he rose to his feet to go outside to relieve himself. He had to step over several bodies to get to the door and had to push James out of the way to get the door opened. It was already early morning and he could hear people up and about getting ready to begin their day. He missed the quietness of Galilee and the sweet smell of the flowers along the lake. Here all he heard were dogs barking, children crying, and people shouting at each other. He couldn't wait to get back home.

They all sat huddle for most of the morning waiting for news. No one had even thought of trying to find something to eat. "What if Peter has gotten arrested also," asked Andrew to everyone but got no response.

After a while, James spoke up. "Why don't we send someone to the Temple area and see what has happened to Peter, and if possible, our teacher?"

Everyone looked around waiting for someone to volunteer but no one seemed to want to. Finally, Nathanael raised his tremoring hand and said that he would do it. They all shook their heads up and down in agreement and Andrew had to help him towards the door. He was painstakingly slow but no one said anything to hurry him up.

"Be careful and watch out for the Romans," cautioned Andrew. "And for God's sake do not tell anyone where we are if you get caught."

Nathanael had not considered being caught by the Romans and that disturbed him. He was about to back out but before he could say anything the door flew open almost hitting him in the face. It was his mother, Mary leaning against the shoulder of the other Mary and both had been crying. "He is dead," she sobbed dropping to her knees. "They have killed my son."

Nathanael's eyes grew wide in terror and he turned to look at the men in the room, all of whom looked white as sheep. "What," asked Andrew? "What do you mean, he's dead?"

The other Mary whose eyes were blurred with tears spoke. "He was crucified," she said. "They had him nailed to a cross." As soon as she said that she began crying again. "We took him down just before coming here."

Then Nathanael noticed John for the first time. "What did you do with the body," he asked John.

"One of the Sanhedrin, Joseph of Arimathea who had spoken for Jesus during the trial, received permission to take his body and place it in his tomb," he answered.

"And that's where he is now," asked Andrew?

"Yes, that is where we placed him."

Suddenly all grew quiet. Then as if an afterthought Nathanael asked, "How about Peter. Have you seen him?"

"Not since the trial," answered John. "He was with me for a time but then ran away after someone spotted him. I haven't seen him since."

A great relief came over Nathanael. "Well, I guess then there's no reason to go looking for him. I'm sure he will be coming back soon."

"If he hasn't been crucified also," said James looking frightened.

"That's enough of that kind of talk," yelped Andrew, his voice betraying his fear. "We will wait until tomorrow and see if we can find him."

Peter came back later that day looking sullen and worn. He had little to say other than he had been identified and had to bolt before being arrested. No one asked him anything else for he looked too mortified to speak. In fact, no one knew what to say. Their Lord had been crucified and now they were alone.

It was evening and they all sat quietly, no one daring to look at each other. Mary Magdala had brought in some food and wine for them but no one ate. Nathanael could not think of anything else. How could it have happened so quickly and without them knowing that it would, he asked himself a hundred times? Gone, he was gone. And that was it. They had crucified him Mary had told them, with two other men as revolutionaries. Jesus a revolutionary? And the Jews were the ones who had forced the issue on the Romans. What in the world had happened?

The Sabbath was spent holding out in the room with little being said to each other and except for the occasional barking of a dog outside the window, little noise was heard. They ate little, most being too sick at their stomachs to eat, and with their backs to the wall they fell in and out of consciousness in utter disbelief. The night was long coming and still, nothing had been said as to what they should do.

Nathanael fell asleep thinking about Jesus but was awoke startled by one of the women yelling something from the courtyard. He jumped up looking for a place to hide when John yelled from the door full of excitement and wonder.

"It's Mary," he yelled to everyone. "She says that Jesus has risen."

"What," said Nathanael? Immediately eyes went searching around the room for an explanation but there was none forthcoming. Nathanael ran to the door followed by James and John. It was early and standing in the courtyard, her arms stretched out towards them was Mary, barely visible in the morning light.

Suddenly Peter came barging through pushing them aside and ran down the steps to Mary grabbing her shoulders. "What do you mean," Nathanael heard him ask unbelievably. "How could he have risen?"

Mary was glowing and it was hard for her to get the words out so instead of trying to talk further Peter looked up at the others as if trying to decide what to do and then without saying a word he let her go and took off running towards the tomb, and right behind him was John.

"Where have they gone," asked Andrew now standing beside the door with Nathanael.

"To the tomb I think," he muttered lightly. "She says that he has risen." Then shaking his head back and forth he added, "Whatever that means."

They waited what seemed forever, expecting Peter to return promptly but as time went by they settled down waiting for the news. Mary had come in to be with Jesus' mother and they sat by themselves at a table speaking lightly to each other and sometimes giggling. Thomas who had been in one of the corners had not said a word all day and suddenly got up and walked to the door. He was visibly shaking and wringing his hands. "I'm going home," he said. "I've had enough of this. You can stay and get arrested, I'm not."

Neither Andrew nor Nathanael who were now outside on the stairs said a word as they watched Thomas walk off. Andrew shook his head and went back inside and then Nathanael after having looked around for Romans walked back through the door following him. The others had already gone in. Nathanael glanced around at everyone but this time, things were different. Every one of them seemed alive again. The fear was still present but there was now as a sense of hope bubbling up throughout the room. It even made him feel hopeful but hopeful for what? Could it be true, he wondered. Could he have risen?

Finally, after a long silence, James spoke. "What do you think that means?" he asked no one in particular. "About having risen?"

"I don't know ask Mary," said Andrew looking around. "Do we dare think that he is alive based on her words?"

"He is risen, I tell you," said Mary excitedly. "I saw him with my own eyes and I looked into the tomb. He was not there."

"I believe her," said his mother. "I am sure that he is alive. He told us that he would come back, don't you remember?"

Nathanael glanced around to see if anyone else seemed to agree with her but no one said a word. Suddenly the door flew open and it was Peter with John right behind him. They were both smiling profusely and Peter was huffing trying to get his breath.

"They were right," he yelled breathing hard, a smile exploding on his bearded face. Then he spotted Mary and ran over to her and kissed her forehead. "You were right Mary," he said lovingly. "Jesus' body is gone. He must be alive. Jesus is alive!"

Everyone was up and coming over to Peter. The two Mary's were hugging each other and everyone was asking questions. "Did you see him," asked James excitedly. "Did you actually see Jesus?"

"No," he said still breathing heavily. "But I saw his tomb and it was empty. And Mary saw him, didn't you Mary? She spoke with him just as she said, didn't he?"

Mary spoke up. "Yes and he told me to tell you to stay here and that he would come to you."

They looked at each other confused but now giddy. "When?" asked Andrew. "Did he say when?"

"No, just for us to go back and wait," she answered.

"Do you believe he has truly risen?" asked Philip.

Peter looked around the room and every eye was on him. "Yes I do," he said excitedly. "Remember when he told us that where he was going we wouldn't be able to follow?" he asked. "Well, I believe now that he was giving us a warning that he would be crucified. And then he said that in a little while and you will no longer see me, and again a little while later and you will see me."

Nathanael's heart pounded as he listened to Peter's words. It was the truth, he knew it was, and the excitement caused by these words was unbearable. "Yes, I remember those words," he shouted loudly immediately regretting that he had done so.

Everyone looked at Nathanael and then back to Peter. "Then he said that our hearts will be in anguish, remember, but then our hearts will rejoice." He looked around at every one of them in awe and then suddenly added. "And haven't our hearts been in anguish?" he said. "And now aren't they filled with joy?"

Everyone began to agree; first James and then Andrew and Philip and Nathanael and then all the rest. Finally, Peter looking around asked, "Where's Thomas?"

Andrew raised his shoulders as if he had no clue. "He said he was going home."

"Well no one else leaves," he commanded, his kind tone suddenly changing. "I'm sure he will come back to check up on us. Until then we stay put until our Lord appears."

The next evening they were all sitting quietly. They had eaten from a pot of venison stew that Mary had found for them and then had prayed for some time, but now they sat in the candlelight looking everywhere but at the door. Peter had locked the doors and placed some furniture in front of them in fear of the Jews and the Romans. "We will be alright," he told them all earlier. "He will come, do not be afraid."

Then suddenly without warning or any sounds, Jesus appeared before them in the middle of the room. John jumped and Philip grabbed Nathanael's arm tightly. They all stared intently at the object in front of them in shock and fear.

He slowly turned around so that they all could see him smiling as only he could do, so as to calm their fears. Then he slowly raised his hands to show them his piercings. "Peace be with you," he said softly but loud enough for everyone to hear.

They all glared at his hands and then he reached for his robe and pulled the seam aside to show his pierced side. No one said a word. Then he said again but a little louder, "Peace be with you. As the Father has sent me, so I send you."

No one moved or said a word. Each had their eyes buried into Jesus' side as they gawked in utter surprise and glee. "Receive the Holy Spirit," he said. "Whose sins you forgive are forgiven them, and whose sins you retain are retained."

Then he was gone. Eyes darted about the room but all was dead quiet. Finally, one of the eleven spoke up. "Was he really there?" asked Andrew looking around the room.

After a long hesitation, John spoke but he was barely perceptible. "Did we really see him, or was he a ghost?"

Then finally Peter spoke. "Certainly it was not a ghost. It was our Lord. He spoke to us, did you not hear him?"

Nathanael watched as they nodded their heads as if to agree. "Now we wait," he added. "We wait until he comes back to tell us where he wants us to go."

"Go where," asked James his eyes wide in anticipation. "Where does he want us to go?"

Peter tried to look certain but his voice failed him. "Well, he didn't say. All he said was that he would be sending us someplace."

Once again they settled down and waited but now there was hope in their movement and joy in their words. Several days later they hear a knock on the door. It startled everyone because no one had come to see them since they had hold up inside and so Peter, who was quickly becoming the leader walked to the door and shouted, "Who is it."

"Thomas," was the answer although barely audible through the door.

"Where have you been Thomas," asked Peter as he dragged him through the door and then after having looked out over the courtyard shut and locked it.

"I was at home," he answered looking around at all the glowing faces. "This place was getting to me."

"Well you're not going to believe what has happened," shouted John his face glowing unlike Thomas had seen it before.

"What," he said immediately. "What's happened? Why is everyone smiling so?"

Then Peter spoke out. "Because we've seen him," he said excitedly. "He has risen."

Thomas looked stupefied. "Who has risen?" he asked.

Peter laughed. "Why our Lord," he shouted. "Our Lord has risen."

"Are you crazy," he lashed out back at Peter. "He's dead. John, you were there. He died on the cross, didn't he? And they buried him. Hundreds saw it. I saw it. He's dead."

John moved forward. "Yes Thomas, you are correct. He did indeed die and he was also buried. But as Peter said, he has risen. We saw him the other night."

"And you're crazy too," he said in reply. "He's dead and you are all crazy."

Then Peter grabbed Thomas' shoulders. "It is true my friend. We've all seen him. I would not lie to you."

Thomas stepped back from his grasp and sneered. "Unless I see the mark of the nails in his hands and put my finger into the nail marks and put my hand into his side, I will not believe." Then he turned and walked over to a corner where he slid down to the floor and placed his head in his arms.

"You shall see my friend," said Peter calmly. "He will come back and then you shall see."

A week later they sat still sacred but still elated at the knowledge that Jesus had risen and promised to come see them again. During that time, Peter had begun sending out different brothers to forage for food and gather water and empty the waste. Nathanael had noted that it had become common to hear Peter shout out orders and then see someone obey them. He didn't really care himself who gave the orders, he just wanted to get out of that room and back to somewhere in Galilee. It had become disheartening having to wait day by day with no more word from Jesus and not knowing what the Jews and the Romans were up to.

That evening Nathanael was talking to Peter about fishing when suddenly Jesus appeared just has he had the time before and in the same spot. "Peace be with you," he said as he had done the other day.

Then he looked around and when he spotted Thomas sitting on the floor he said, "Get up." Thomas did, wide-eyed and shaking. Jesus showed him his hands. "Put your finger here and see my hands, and bring your hand and put it into my side, and do not be unbelieving, but believe."

Thomas fell to his knees crying and shouted, "My Lord and my God."

Then Jesus placed his hand on Thomas' shoulder and raised him up and said, "Have you come to believe because you have seen me, Thomas? Blessed are those who have not seen and have believed."

Then each, in turn, touched the wounds of Jesus. Finally, his mother came over to him and instead of touching the wounds she kissed him on the cheek. Even Mary Magdala refused to touch the wounds but instead laughed with joy. He then took bread and broke it and gave each one a piece and together they ate it.

After telling the Apostles to go back to Galilee and wait there, they packed what belongings they could take without being obvious to the Romans and left the next day. It would take them five days to reach Peter's home town which they did without incident. And then they waited.

Chapter 18 – Tiberius

It wasn't until Antipas arrived in Tiberius that he found out that Herodias had returned. She was waiting for him in the courtyard and as he entered she came to him quickly and gave him a healthy hug and kiss. It surprised Antipas for he had been certain that she would never set foot in Tiberius again, much less do it with a kiss. Not only did she welcome him with open arms but next to the pool was a small feast of duck, venison, nuts, bread, and plenty of wine.

"Welcome home my love," her voice high in anticipation. She was wearing his favorite gown that was cut very suggestively in many places. "I was wondering if you were ever coming home."

Antipas did not know what to say. The last few days had taken a toll on him and his ride back from Jerusalem had been accompanied by many bad dreams. But now a huge burden seemed to have been lifted. "It is good to be home and even better to have you here to greet me," he said carefully, still not trusting her in the least. Seductive or not, she could still be as dangerous as a black widow spider.

"And why should I not be," she said giggling. "Quick," she said turning her head to find a servant. "Bring my husband a cup of wine." She then turned back to him. "I want to hear all about your visit to Jerusalem but first, let us feast some for I am famished and I and sure you are."

He was indeed hungry for they had not eaten the entire day. "You are right, I am hungry. It all looks delicious."

After eating they sat on the patio upstairs overlooking the city and admiring the lights in the sky. She had had a lot of wine to drink and was starting to slur her words but he paid no care. He was just happy to have peace in his house for once.

"Tell me," she asked. "What happened to that preacher that was baptized by John? I understand that he went to Jerusalem. Did you see him?"

Suddenly his mood changed. In one swift instant, she had destroyed his peace and brought back the melancholy that he had carried with him for the last week. "They crucified him," he said trying to sound as if it meant nothing to him.

With those words, she shot straight up dropping her cup on the floor spraying red wine across the tiles all the way over to his couch. He frowned at the mess. "You killed him?" she asked.

"No, not me," he countered heavily, his voice rising in defense of himself. "I didn't have anything to do with it. It was Pilate. He's the one that murdered the poor man."

She leaned back down on her couch and looked up into the sky. "These two men, who somehow were connected to each other, ended up in horrible deaths. I wonder why?"

"It really doesn't matter dear," he said after taking a deep drink from his cup. The wine was one of his favorites and he expected to drink much that night, with or without her. "They are both dead and neither will be remembered for very long. They were both interesting and amusing in their own ways but neither did very much to be remembered for."

"Not like you, my love," she said still gazing at the night sky. "You will always be remembered."

"Yes," he said after a pause but not too convincing. "Just like my father before me."

It was the last thing he heard from her for she began to snore slightly and he knew that she would not wake up until morning. So much for the romantic evening she had proposed to him earlier. As he looked up at the stars he wondered what people would think about him after he had been dead and buried. Would they remember him as a good king, he wondered or as a tyrant as his father had really been. And then his mind fell back to John and the many weeks they had spent in the dungeon together talking about the afterlife and God. What in the world could lead a man to give up everything to follow such as a life? He had accomplished nothing but to relieve himself of his head. And it was this Jesus that he had been sent to heralded he had told him one evening. It was he and not John that had meant something to the world. It was this Jesus that would save us from our sins; he tried to explain, and looked where it got him. He, like John, was now dead and they were both rotting in their graves.

Antipas stood up and poured himself another cup of wine. "Yes, they will be forgotten," he said out loud to know one for he was now all alone. "And I will be remembered."

The next day a dispatch was handed to him by a Roman carrier who waited just outside the door for a reply just in case there was one. It was from Pilate which surprised him. Why would he send a note so soon after they had just spent the entire evening with each other? Antipas had a headache from too much wine the night before and this didn't help. He sat down and broke the seal. In it was a parchment with these words on it:

THE BODY OF JESUS IS MISSING. MY MEN SAY THAT HIS FOLLOWERS ARE CLAIMING THAT INSTEAD OF HAVEN TAKEN HIM FROM HIS TOMB, THAT HE HAS RISEN FROM THE DEAD. CAN YOU BELIEVE THAT?

WE HAVE INFORMATION THAT THESE FOLLOWERS OF HIS HAVE GONE BACK TO GALILEE. I WANT THAT BODY BACK BEFORE I HAVE AN INSURRECTION ON MY HANDS, WHICH I WILL BE FORCED, NO DOUBT, TO PUT

THE BLAME ON YOU. FIND THEM AND FIND THE BODY
AND CONTACT ME AS SOON AS YOU HAVE DONE SO.

PILATE

Immediately Antipas' lip began to twitch.

Names and Places

Galilee – Provence of Roman in ancient Israel north of Jerusalem and east of the Sea of Galilee ruled by Herod Antipas.

Perea – Provence of Rome to the east of Jerusalem and north of the Dead Sea also ruled by Herod Antipas.

Herod Antipas – Tetrarch of Galilee and Perea and grandson of Herod the Great

Herodias - wife of Antipas and granddaughter of Herod the Great

Salome – daughter of Herodias and stepdaughter of Antipas

Valerius Gratus – first Prefect of Judea before Pontius Pilate

Pontius Pilate – second Prefect of Judea.

Manaen – close friend of Antipas

Abda - servant of Herodias

Claudia - wife of Pontius Pilate

John – The Baptizer

Nathanael – disciple of John and later of Jesus

Joanna - the wife of one of Antipas' stewards

Herod II – former husband of Herodias and Antipas' half-brother

Phasaelis – ex-wife of Herod Antipas and the daughter of King Aretas IV

Tiberius – the capital of Galilee built and ruled by Herod Antipas

Phillip I – the Tetrarch of Iturea (north of Galilee) who is betrothed to Salome

Machaerus – the capital of Perea ruled by Antipas and where John is beheaded

Sepphoris – Town to the east of Tiberius in Galilee

High Priest Caiaphas – High priest of Judea at time of Jesus' death

Gennesaret – a small fishing town on the Sea of Galilee

Historical Explanations

Almost all of the history of Jesus comes from the 27 books and letters of the New Testament of the Bible. But it must be remembered that the gospels are not a chronological history of Jesus' life, but are divine inspiring accounts of bits and pieces of his life, his sayings, and his miracles. Many of the accounts of the gospels are told differently, some differ in sequences, some not told at all in the other gospels, and even some contradicting each other. But they are all inspired and give us a true picture of the short life of Jesus as he lived it.

Along with the New Testament, other historical references can also be found outside the Bible. Herod Antipas, for instance, who is barely mentioned in the New Testament, was indeed the king (or Tetrarch as called by the Romans) of Galilee and Perea and that he ruled for over thirty years there having inherited his kingdom from his father Herod the Great. He was known for building great cities (Tiberius was his most renown) and ruling over a relatively peaceful province as compared to his half-brother who ruled over Judea. Having divorced his wife, Phasaelis, the daughter of King Aretas IV, Herod Antipas seduces Herodias (the wife of his half-brother Herod II, who was Tetrarch of Judea). Herod II dies soon afterward and the Roman Empire appoints first Valerius Gratus as the first Prefect of Judea and then later Pontius Pilate, instead of assigning another Herod to be a Tetrarch of that province. This novel takes place shortly after the appointment of Pontius Pilate as Prefect of Judea.

John the Baptizer (or also known as the Baptist) is taken from the New Testament of the Bible and can be found in all four gospels. In Matthew and Luke, his story of being beheaded at a birthday party of Herod Antipas is told and later referenced by the Roman historian Josephus. The gospels state that John attacked Herod Antipas' marriage as contrary to Jewish law and that it was incestuous, as Herodias was also Antipas' niece. Josephus also points out that John criticized the fact that Herodias was also his brother's wife (see Mark 6:18), lending credence to the belief that Antipas and Herodias married while Herod II was still alive.

Some historians have John imprisoned by Antipas in his palace of Machaerus in Perea while others say that he was imprisoned in Tiberius in Galilee. The name of the city is not mentioned in the Bible. I opt towards Machaerus for the sake of the novel. Either way, John is executed and according to the gospels of Matthew and Mark, Herod was reluctant to order John's death because he liked him but was compelled by Herodias' daughter, to whom he had promised any reward she chose as a result of her dancing for guests at his birthday banquet.

Philip the first, married his niece Salome, the daughter of Herodias and Herod II (sometimes referred to as Herod Philip I).

This person Salome appears in the Bible only in connection with the execution of John the Baptist. The gospels of Matthew and Mark state that the Herodias whom Herod Antipas married was the wife of Antipas' brother "Philip", but according to the Roman historian Josephus, she was the wife of another half-brother, Herod II. I have opted to go with the version that Salome is the daughter of Herodias and Herod II and it was her that convinced her stepfather Herod Antipas to behead John the Baptist as described in Matthew.

The name Nathanael is referenced only from the book of John in the New Testament of the Bible and is not listed in the other three synoptic gospels (Matthew, Mark, and Luke). The Nathanael of John's gospel appears to parallel the apostle Bartholomew found in the other three gospels, as both are paired with Philip in the respective gospels. I have decided to call Bartholomew by John's name Nathanael. It is Nathanael whom Jesus tells that he saw him sitting under a fig tree which made Nathanael fall to his knees and proclaimed, "Rabbi, you are the son of God; you are the King of Israel."

This story ends with the crucifixion of Jesus and his resurrection as witnessed by the Apostles, Mary Magdala, Mary, the mother of Jesus, and many others. There is no doubt that he was seen by hundreds of witnesses who saw him after he had risen.

Bibliography

Daily Life at the Time of Jesus' – Miriam Vamosh

Josephus' *Jewish Antiquities* - Herodias' divorce and marriage to Antipas

Catholic Companion Edition New American Bible

Gospel of Matthew - various passages on the life of Jesus and the Apostles

Gospel of Mark - various passages on the life of Jesus and the Apostles

Gospel of John - various passages on the life of Jesus and the Apostles

Gospel of Luke - various passages on the life of Jesus and the Apostle

Dolorous Passion of Our Lord Jesus Christ' – Anne Catherine Emmerich

Wikipedia – History and dynasty, biblical names, clothing of ancient times, wildlife and cuisine.

Other books by Robert Holladay that can be found on Amazon Kindle:

'The Gods are No More'

'The Arrows of Glywysing' (book 2 in the Gods are No More series)

'Lands of the Visigoths' (book 3 in the Gods are No More series)

'William' the story of a homeless man

'The Map'

'The Boboli Gardens'

Thank you for reading my books. I hope you enjoy some of them. Please take a few moments to rate this book on Amazon if you liked it.

https://www.amazon.com/s/ref=nb_sb_noss_1?url=node%3D154606011&field-keywords=robert+holladay

Made in the USA
Lexington, KY
16 January 2017